A04 008 688 7

Hitherto
Christina Chitenderu
ISBN: 978-1-8384686-3-7

The right of Christina Chitenderu to be identified as the author of this work has been asserted in accordance with the Copyright Designs and Patents Act 1988.

A copy of this book is deposited with the British Library

Published By: -

i2i

P U B L I S H I N G

i2i Publishing. Manchester.
www.i2ipublishing.co.uk

Hitherto

A journey of courage despite the odds.

The genesis of the land reform programme in Zimbabwe attracted sanctions being imposed on the nation. The once breadbasket of Africa experienced a mudslide in the economy characterised by an enormous rise in inflation, with salaries remaining stagnant. Aneni, a young girl with big dreams, wanted to flee the country to the United Kingdom in the hope that she could help her loving family. As the chances of sponsorship appeared bleak, Aneni sought to jump the border into Mozambique on foot. With nothing but a rucksack and a small bag, she hoped to raise money and fulfil her dream. A perilous journey began, with Aneni resorting to masquerading under a false identity in order to be accepted in society.

4

Acknowledgements

the Lord above for giving me the strength. My late parents Samuel and Rose for always believing in me. That spirit keeps me going. I hear their voices when I'm about to give up. My siblings Bertha, Helen, late Barbs, Emanuel, Kenneth, Verna, Chitsva, Josephine and Rashma for always standing by me. To my village of strong women who desist from giving up on me and keep encouraging me Mahali, Linda, Nyaradzo, Elizabeth, Elsa, Samantha, aunt Charity, thank you.

To the love of my life, my daughter Tanya. You give mummy strength all the time, words fail me for the strong young woman you're becoming.

Introduction

Hitherto seeks to restore hope on the counter existence of migration, destroying the illusion that people only want to mutiny. It addresses the challenges faced by migrants, tackling the push factors like war, hunger, economic crisis, and political instability.

Although there are different categories of migration, this book will explore the challenges faced by poor migrants who, due to poverty, have no resources to migrate legally. As a result, they tend to use clandestine ways of crossing the borders in search of a better life. However, travel is only the first step of the journey, as people seek acceptance in places that don't want them. *Hitherto* outlines the subjection to stereotypes, stigma and discrimination of migrants.

The journey of migration has often been presented with loneliness and desperation, showcasing the raw human will to survive. This book will highlight the boldness one needs to pursue their dreams even in the most difficult circumstances.

Chapter 1

A dark, cold blanket hung across the sky. It threatened to rain, but Aneni was beaming with happiness that seemed to erase all the gloominess.

"Mummy, mummy, I passed! Look at my report card! I came second in class!" she screamed the words happily, sweat gushing from her brow after a significantly long run from the school. She desperately wanted her family to know that her efforts had paid off.

Aneni had come second in her Grade 1 class. This was after repeating the grade as she had not done very well the first time. In the previous year, she was not yet confident in her abilities and, in a composition about describing oneself, Aneni ended up copying a fellow pupil's work word for word, including their first names and surname. Needless to say, she did not get a good grade for that assignment.

Aneni was the fifth born out of a family of seven. She had three brothers: Mandebvu was the eldest, followed by Maguza, the second born and then Kulenyu the third born. Her three sisters were Madanha, the eldest sister and fourth born followed by, Mudiwa the fifth who came before Aneni, and then Anesu, the last born.

Aneni's family were subsistence farmers, with maize and groundnuts being the main crops. Her mother, Mama Mushambi, had had training in adult literacy and very often would teach adults at Rowa Primary School in the Manicaland province of Zimbabwe. It was the same primary school that Aneni went to. Sadly, the adult literacy classes were not very consistent in attendance as some parents were too occupied to go, especially during the planting season.

MaMushambi was dedicated and committed to her role as an adult literacy teacher even though the remuneration was not great. She was a very soft-spoken, loving and humble woman, and she always brought the family together. She never engaged in arguments or confrontations, advocating instead for dialogue to solve any family disagreements.

"Well done, Ane, my beautiful daughter," her mama said while taking her warm, loving arms. There was a twinkle of pride and happiness in Aneni's eyes, and she saw the pride reflected in her mother's gaze. Aneni rejoiced and felt a sense of achievement when she made her parents smile. Equally, her parents felt a sense of pride when their children achieve their best. They felt that they had done a good job. Pride is an accolade, an emotional medal that can only be felt from within, bringing fullness into their hearts.

It wasn't a secret that Aneni's father, VaMushambi enjoyed the drink. Most of the afternoons, after doing farm work, he would go to the local village shops to drink with his friends and return home later in the evenings. On this day when he returned, he was greeted by the news that Aneni had passed her grade. VaMushambi embraced his daughter and congratulated her, saying that she was smart and could soar even higher if she worked hard.

The following day, VaMushambi brought Aneni a packet of Charhons biscuits, a popular brand of cookies in the 1980s that children in Zimbabwe enjoyed very much. In that era, Zimbabwe dripped milk and honey - food security, education and the health systems were impeccably great. Life was abundant. Schools in rural areas were almost free, and the government supported farmers by providing them with seed, fertilisers, and training on how to yield a bumper harvest.

The biscuits came in a 20-unit pack, which Aneni decided to share with her siblings who had also celebrated her success. And just like that, the holidays had begun in the most cheerful way. Aneni was extremely excited as she had something good to brag about to her cousins who were supposed to visit them for holidays.

Rowa was a dynamic village, with most families living on subsistence farming. Only a few households had fathers who worked in the city and would return home to their families for holidays or weekends. It was rare to find women who worked other jobs besides farming. Their role was to take care of the children and keep the homes running. The chores for women included fetching water and firewood, cooking, and cleaning the house. Water sources were available at the local school boreholes and dams. However, due to health concerns, the Health Department advised the communities to only use water from the boreholes for drinking and cooking. The water from the dams and rivers was considered perfectly fine for bathing and doing laundry, but not for consumption. Since Aneni's family didn't have running water, the women in the family had to get accustomed to using their heads to balance water cans. They didn't live in luxury, but they were not extremely poor.

Their farm was very big, and firewood was abundant. Very often, other residents from the reserves would come and fetch it. In some instances, people got tired of asking for permission, and they helped themselves to the firewood.

"After all, the Mushambis are very nice people, they will not complain," the people would say.

Aneni's home had no electricity - they used candles and paraffin lamps for lighting. She learnt to fetch firewood at a tender age. Oh, how she wished that her family had an electric stove, but it was always fun getting firewood with her mum and sisters, so she didn't complain often. They did not have much in terms of material possessions, but Aneni's life was full of love and laughter. One of her hobbies was playing netball at school. When they had interschool competitions, MaMushambi and VaMushambi would come to watch her play. That gesture melted her heart because, in those days, it was a rare occurrence, especially for fathers, to be involved in their children's extracurricular activities. As her parents cheered for her, she thought to herself, *I would do anything to make them happy.*

Religion was also a big part of Aneni's upbringing. The family were active members of the United Methodist Church, attending service almost every Sunday. The church building was local, with smaller branches within a three to six kilometre radius. MaMushambi was especially an active member of the church, with pivotal roles which she executed with dedication and immense commitment. The community noticed her devotion, consistently re-nominating her for the role of church elder. MaMushambi was a great leader. She listened more than she talked, and she made decisions that helped people around her. Aneni's dad, on the other hand, never attended church. He preferred to be out, enjoying a traditional brew with other men of the village. However, every evening after supper, the family would gather to sing church hymns and pray. This inspired Aneni to follow the religious path in life, letting it be her moral compass .The family would sit in the kitchen every evening and religiously sing and pray before going to bed, which gave birth to Aneni's passion for hymn songs.

In Grade 5, Aneni was in the school choir at Rowa Primary School. On one occasion, her music teacher, Mr Simango, heard the children making discord in the choir and asked Aneni to sing a solo as he thought she was the one missing the note. After singing the solo, Mr Simango said in vernacular, "Ndiko kunozi kuimbaka uku." *this is what we call singing*, "she sings like a Negro". Of course, her head grew big and she became the envy of the group. At that time, most people did not understand the connotations of the word "Negro" to racial injustice and slavery in America. They simply thought it meant black *American*. The black *Americans* were known to have rich, rounded and impeccable singing voices.

In her youth, Aneni was an active member of the United Methodist Youth Fellowship, also known as UMYF in the local church. This fellowship involved attending revivals, meetings and several youth programmes. It brought a sense of independence and responsibility to teenage Aneni. It also made her realise how important it was to work hard and give back to her community.

The community had many forms of beliefs and traditions, for example an event called *Mademba*. *Mademba* took place after a period of dry spells. Some practised what was called winter ploughing, which prepared the land for planting season before the rains. *Mademba* involved people gathering in a place that was decided by the village head called *Sabhuku* or chief called *Mambo*. People would request the ancestors to bring the rains which would guarantee a bumper harvest. A local beer would be brewed seven days prior to the ceremony and the villagers would try to also appease the ancestors by pouring a few drops on the land.

Most of the time when this process was done, the clouds would begin to gather in the sky and drops of rain would begin to fall. Beliefs remain a mystery that is only understood by the people who believe in them. In essence, this enabled villagers to have confidence in their ancestral powers by communicating with them. There is a lot of discourse on how some communities had more faith in their ancestral guidance than God. Somehow, even the staunch Christians still participated in traditional activities. Without looking much into the complexity of beliefs, such activities simply brought the community a feeling of oneness. The spirit of Hunhu - humanity - made people come together despite their differences. The oneness surpassed extreme differences. Even people who had destroyed other people's relationships through adultery, or who had stolen someone else's crops would put all that aside and focus on the more pressing issues.

When she was thirteen, Aneni realised that boys were beginning to notice her. They called her beautiful, even offering her gifts and candy. This of course was a natural part of growing up as it was inevitable for young people to start looking at each other in a different, more mature way. What mattered was how they reacted to this new kind of attention and how they navigated new relationships.

MaMushambi took an open approach in addressing love and relationships. She always advised Aneni and her siblings on how important it was to remain chaste until marriage. She focused on empowering young girls and telling them to learn and discover who they were without distraction from the boys. However, she made sure not to scare the girls or tell them to suppress their feelings. She used her famous motto: *books before boys.* It was supposed to reinforce and encourage young people to get an education before they indulge in or commit to relationships. Aneni was free to talk to her mum if boys had approached her or when she had developed an interest in a particular boy. This open-door approach helped to create an open platform for MaMushambi to give advice to her daughters. Aneni embraced and yearned to follow the rules as she believed that her mum had valid reasons and knowledge to guide her in the right way. Her words were always consistent with the biblical principles that youth at church were advised to follow, so she had to be correct.

Aneni's parents modelled a loving relationship, which helped them raise their children in a stable home. Her parents would even eat together from the same plate. They would wake up early in the morning, while it was still peacefully quiet, with only the sound of birds chirping and singing beautiful melodies, to chat and laugh before a hard day's work. They would discuss the successes and mischiefs of their children as well as dreams for their future. After the morning chat, MaMushambi would always be heard opening the bedroom door before going out to stand on the veranda. Aneni's father would stand next to her, commenting on the weather and checking on their crops.

"Mmm, a lot of dew there is today. And there are footprints in the yard. They look like dog's paws, but they appear bigger than those of our dogs," VaMushambi would mumble as he walked to the girls' quarters to wake them up. Scratching his head out of habit other than anything else, VaMushambi would say in a hoarse voice, "Who could cause the footprints? Ahh, maybe it's these witches who move about the night when they should be sleeping." Aneni and her sisters would giggle in response.

"It's probably just the wild animals moving about at night", MaMushambi would say.

"I still think it's the witches. I heard something when I went to use the toilet at night and-," VaMushambi would counter.

Conversations between the two would always start with the weather and end up being about something totally different. Sometimes witchcraft, sometimes wild animals roaming around, or just harmless gossip. They would talk and talk until it was time to get their children ready.

Aneni was not keen on doing farm work. She enjoyed staying at home cleaning the house and preparing food while everyone else went to the fields. However, there were days when MaMushambi would call everyone to go to the fields and, inevitably, Aneni had no choice but to go. This part of her upbringing made Aneni warm up to embracing a diversity of chores and accepting that, sometimes one had to work hard to have a comfortable life.

Life for Aneni was quite dynamic growing up, but love... love was consistent!

Chapter 2

In 1994, Aneni finished Grade 7, and her journey at Rowa Primary School ended on a high note. She had secured a place at Biriiri Mission, a boarding school in the Chimanimani area, about sixty kilometres away from home. The school belonged to the United Baptist Church, and it was run on the principles of Christianity. One of her brothers, Maguza, the second born in the family, was doing very well economically at the time, so he took it upon himself to pay for Aneni's school fees and all other expenses associated with the school.

"Education is worth everything," he had told her. He bought everything new, and for the first time, Aneni used bed sheets. In the village, going to boarding school was a big achievement, and it dramatically changed one's position on the social strata. The emotion and excitement of living boarding life overwhelmed her. She was, of course, excited about learning new things at a renowned establishment, but she couldn't stop thinking about the people she would meet and the places she would see. She simply couldn't wait to get there.

The first day at boarding school was characterised by curiosity, shock, competition and a clash of different social classes. It was a moment of navigating where one wanted to and could fit in with little to no effort. Yes, Aneni was from a village, from a house with no electricity and tap water, let alone a television. However, she liked hanging out with the cream from affluent backgrounds. In no time, she had gained a refined accent. Most students who came from affluent backgrounds had a peculiar accent because of their exposure to multi-racial primary schools and plush environments. The assimilation was so quick and easy that most students thought she also came from one of the affluent suburbs. She did not correct them.

Trying to fit into a certain class came with its own challenges: during socialisation some things started not to add up. For example, it became uncomfortable for Aneni to talk about television programmes as she didn't know any when most of her affluent friends would discuss movies, series and other exciting TV programmes. She would resort to attentively listening and re-relating as if she had watched the programmes herself. It was a hard task to follow and a tough act to maintain, but she managed. The quality of her clothes also became a hint that she didn't fit in as they did not exactly match affluence. However, that did not deter Aneni from continuing to mingle amongst the students of more prosperous backgrounds.

Biriiri was a great school as the teachers were dedicated to making students achieve the best. The whole school religiously attended church on Sundays. Some Sundays were vibrant, while others were relaxed. Students especially loved the harvest Sundays because the community would bring fresh maize and *ipwa* -sweet reeds- to share with the students. It was indeed a treat, especially mid-term, when all the goodies brought from home had since vanished, relying solely on dining meals. The patter of happy feet that had welcomed them in the first week of school was gone. During this time, students would slowly drag their feet to the dining hall because they had goodies and snacks to munch on in-between school meals.

The first year at Biriiri was bliss, and it was very consistent with what Aneni had envisioned. Her second year went well until the last term, when Aneni's brother, the sponsor of her education, lost his job. The company his brother Maguza was working for had suddenly gone into administration, which meant loss of jobs for the workers The family wanted to protect her and let her focus on her studies, so they did not explain much to her about what had happened. They probably thought the situation was going to get better soon, and they would never have to tell her how close she came to being withdrawn from the school she loved so much. The prospect of shame and the likelihood of the community laughing at their situation made her family fearful.

The days that followed were nothing short of a nightmare. She got sent home regularly for fees but would return with nothing. She was sent home a dozen times until she could not go anymore because she had no money to pay the bus fare. It was also difficult for Aneni to see the pain in her parents' eyes, especially MaMushambi's, each time she returned home. With full knowledge that the money was not there, the pain was too hard to bear, and she couldn't do anything to make it go away.

Several times, she would opt to travel at night so that she would get home while it was dark when no one in the community could see her. She would even stay at home, avoiding going to the shops. At one point, while she was home for school fees, her aunt came to visit for the whole weekend, and Aneni did not want her aunt to notice that she was home during term time. She had to come up with a strategy whether her parents were comfortable with it or not.

At Aneni's farm, there was another small house that was separate from their main house. It was not regularly used for daily operations, but it was sometimes used to store farm equipment. She stayed there, and her mum would bring her food to that little house. Her mum was against the idea of her daughter alienating herself. However, Aneni felt too much shame to show herself to anyone.

There were times when she would stay at the dormitory during study periods at school so that the school management would not find her. Unfortunately, the school management was informed by the school matron that Aneni was still in school even after being sent home for school fees. This time she had no option but to go home.

Aneni couldn't force herself to go home again, so she got an idea. Her maternal grandmother, Mary, lived in Chakohwa, about forty kilometres away from the school. Instead of going back home, Aneni took a bus up to an area called Wengezi and walked to her maternal grandmother's home. The distance was about fifteen kilometres. It was at the peak of summer, and she had no money. She walked on foot in the scorching sun, sweating under her school uniform. People who saw her walk by probably assumed that she was not planning to walk very far. Some looks were full of concern, but Aneni wore a face of confidence, appearing as if everything, except the scorching sun, was perfectly fine. She arrived at her grandmother's house and found her preparing beans for sale. Chakohwa area had benefited from irrigation schemes by the government, and this made farming of certain produce, such as beans, perennial.

Grandma saw Aneni, hugged her, and with a voice full of concern said, "Come, let's sit on the mat." Aneni immediately told her grandmother why she was there- the school fees issue- and how she could not bear to see her parents' worried faces. She added that she wanted to return to school the following day and needed money for bus fare. Aneni could see that her grandmother did not have the money, but she smiled anyway, not wanting to cause any more worry.

God must have heard Aneni's prayers and responded quite quickly. That same night, Aneni's aunt, Nakai, came from the capital city of Harare to visit grandma. Aneni was filled with immense excitement at the thought of her getting some money for her bus fare. The following morning, Aunt Nakai gave her a twenty dollar note. In those days, twenty Zimbabwean dollars was quite a substantial amount. It bore on it an elephant, perhaps depicting its grandiose capacity. The money was going to suffice for her immediate need.

As Aneni was leaving her grandma's place, grandma pulled her into a hug.

"Stay strong. One day everything will be alright," she said. The heart-warming words gave Aneni the strength she needed to go back to school. At fifteen, Aneni learnt to accept difficulties as part of life, and to think on her feet. She was the epitome of bravery and the sheer willpower that she possessed.

While on the bus to school, Aneni thoroughly reflected on her situation. She decided to meet with the school management and ask them to give her a grace period as her situation was not getting better. Her parents still had hope that it would improve soon, but she did not.

She got to school, went straight to the reception and asked the school administrator to let the school head know that she wanted to speak to him. The school administrator returned from the head's office and said that the headmaster could see her the following day after assembly. For some strange reason, Aneni held no fear, as in her mind, she was already considering plan B, going to a day school.

In the school, other students noticed management's interest in Aneni. Word had gone out that she had squandered school fees. Some even said that she was in the school's black book now. The black book was a hardcover exercise book in which the head listed students who had committed an offence or had caused serious trouble in the school. So, yes - it was big. The gossip spread like wildfire, and Aneni knew that, whether if it was true or not, everyone believed it. At the tender age of fifteen, Aneni learnt to be calm in the face of adversity. She decided not to focus on the rumours as she knew the truth. Society has been constructed by people making assumptions and coming to conclusions too quickly. It took bold objectivity for people to dig deeper, establish facts and find the truth, and most people didn't have that objectivity. *The danger of a single story* was that it remained singular, and there was no in-between. It conditioned people to think or make assumptions based on a one-sided ideology or stereotype. They didn't know the other side, and they didn't want to know either.

At that time, what Aneni needed was empathy, love and support. She had friends who used to like her, but most of them had fled to avoid being connected to the rumours. It didn't surprise her: no one wanted to be associated with someone who squanders their own school fees.

She was, however, surprised when one of her classmates took her aside.

"Have you tried Social Welfare?" she asked. This simple gesture was so full of kindness that Aneni smiled. Most of the students figured out or were in the process of figuring out her lies about the affluence that she tried to portray at school. She kept her head high, even though she wanted nothing more than to hide from the curious eyes.

Soon after assembly, Aneni strode confidently to the administration office to attend the meeting. Although she was not afraid, the presence of two other senior teachers immediately sent shivers down her spine. At the time, she had thought the meeting would only be with the school head, Mr Dube, who presented calm, understanding and empathetic leadership qualities. She had not expected the meeting to be attended by three senior officials of the school. She looked at the deputy head teacher who was known for being so tough that every student feared him, and she started praying in her mind. The other senior teacher was the deputy head assistant, who also presented a strict demeanour, although he was more compromising than the deputy head teacher.

This is it, Aneni thought to herself. *I will be sent home.* When she entered the office, as intimidated as she was, she had to remind herself why she was there and what her ultimate goal was.

The head teacher gave the floor for Aneni to relate her story, and for a split second, she stumbled over her words. She took a deep breath, detailed her situation, and requested a grace period. She also mentioned that during the said grace period, she would evaluate the situation and, if the problem persisted, she would consider transferring to a day school. The head teacher requested for her to wait outside while they deliberated on the matter.

After about fifteen minutes, the school receptionist asked Aneni to go back to the head's office. The head teacher immediately said, "We have heard and understood your situation. We will let you continue with your studies until the end of the year. If nothing changes until then, we will have to send you home."

It was the second term of her third year, and it was pertinent that this issue be addressed quickly as she was approaching her Ordinary Level examinations. The decision from the management brought a sigh of temporary relief to Aneni. At least she did not have to worry about being sent home for a little while.

Sometimes in life, it didn't only rain - it poured. As if the issue with school fees wasn't enough trouble, two weeks later, Aneni got injured, dislocating her ankle while running to leave the dormitory keys at the matron's house. She tripped over the washing line and fell. She went to the local clinic, but they did not have suitable equipment to nurse the leg, so Aneni was sent to the general hospital with a pair of crutches. Luckily, she got a ride in the school truck, so she did not need to pay.

Her parents suffered with her, realising that their little princess was going through a lot at a very tender age. Unfortunately, they could not afford to even send her to the doctor. Early morning the following day, MaMushambi went to the church treasurer and tried to borrow money, so that they could take Aneni to Mutare General Hospital.

"I'm so sorry to hear that your daughter is nursing a leg. Life is so unpredictable. We send our children to school, but we do not know at all what can befall them when they are there. At least she continues to breathe," remarked MaMudada, the church treasurer.

"Yes, it is a difficult time for us, and we surely need your prayers. The devil is always at work, especially where God is about to bless," MaMushambi responded with much concern but also with impatience as she needed to know whether the treasurer could help her or not. For some reason, MaMudada appeared pompous. The fact that she had keys to open a door for a church member's wellbeing made her feel very important. She compared herself to a saviour in her mind, but never out loud.

Finally, after a lot of bubbling conversation, which MaMushambi was the least interested in, MaMudada went to her coffers and brought out a wad of Zimbabwean dollars. She carefully selected from the wad and handed over two ten-dollar notes to MaMushambi.

"Please, let us know how the child feels and when you can return the money," she said. MaMushambi rushed home to prepare Aneni for the hospital. Aneni was treated without any other issues. She did seem to struggle to walk with crutches, which had been recommended by the physiotherapist, but she learnt how to use them very quickly.

She went back to school after two weeks and was happy to be back. Her friends covered her cast with lovely messages, wishing Aneni a speedy recovery. Some of the teachers wrote on it too, and she felt the warm feeling of love in her heart. Aneni took advantage of the situation as she quite often chose not to attend class and do her work in the dormitory. She soon became friends with many prefects, who were looking for an excuse to stay in the dormitories during the study period, especially during the evening classes. In most cases, students would only concentrate on their studies for the first thirty minutes, and after that, they would start writing letters home or doodling in their notebooks.

One evening, Aneni looked around the room of her caring friends and thought, *there are positives that can come from negatives.* She had never felt so much love from so many people like when she was nursing her leg.

Days and weeks passed, and after a month, Aneni's cast was taken off, and her leg had healed completely. She wrote home to tell her parents that she was fine and that she looked forward to seeing them on holiday. Life went back to normal, but Aneni was shocked at how disappointed she was that the healing of her leg had come at a price. As the cast fell off, so did the attention she had enjoyed when she nursed her dislocated leg. The thought surprised her, and she just laughed it off.

Chapter 3

In 1997, at the end of the third term of form three, Aneni packed her things to go home like everyone else. She looked around and felt a tear in the corner of her eye. Deep inside, she knew that this was farewell and, as painful as it was for her to imagine starting school elsewhere, she realised that only a miracle could make her family afford fees that were already three terms in arrears. However, she let herself hold a little hope and left an empty trunk at the school, hoping to come back at least one more time to pick it up.

During the holidays, the sun would rise high and set gracefully. There was no discussion about fees. Aneni enjoyed the holiday, playing with friends and telling them all about the exciting experiences of boarding school. But as she talked, she lacked confidence and held fear- fear of how her friends would react when they learnt that she could not return to the boarding school that she praised so much. One of her friends, Kero, was enthralled by her stories.

"I wish I had the same privilege as you, Aneni," she said.

"Oh yes, Kero, it is so nice there, and you get to meet people from different walks of life. It is sometimes hard to keep up with the demands of boarding life," Aneni said, kicking a rock in front of her.

"Well, you are already meeting all the people and you are managing so well! You probably can't wait to go back there. I know I would," Kero said with a voice full of confidence. She allowed Kero to think that it was true, letting the dream of going back seem real, even if it was just for a couple of minutes.

The days that followed became monotonous and characterised by many household chores. She also helped out in the fields. The planting rains were on time-a mix of spontaneous downpours and incessant rains- and the sleeping grasslands sprang back to life. Farmers often planted before Christmas time as the rain was abundant in that month. Aneni would help her parents in the morning and sometimes in the evening, but deep inside she knew that she was supposed to be doing something else. Something more decisive!

On a beautiful Tuesday morning at the beginning of the year, Aneni packed her bags to catch a bus that would take eight ours to arrive at a district called Gokwe. The family sat together and prayed for her the night before she embarked on her journey. At four in the morning, while it was still dark and serenely quiet, MaMushambi and VaMushambi escorted Aneni to the bus stop. Both parents gave her their blessings, and off she went.

Her eldest sister Madanha lived in Gokwe, where she worked as a nurse. Madanha lived with her husband, Nevermind, who worked as a deputy head teacher at the local primary school. They lived with their three beautiful children, two boys and a lovely little girl. Zimbabwe was well known for very peculiar names such as Knowledge, Opportunity or Reason. All these names carried a particular meaning for the parents or family, and it didn't matter how unconventional they sounded to a foreign ear.

Another addition to the family was brother-in-law Nevermind's nephew, Wisdom, who was attending primary school at the same school that he was working as the deputy head teacher.

Her sister Madanha and brother in-law had taken on a family philanthropic role, trying to help and support family members from both sides. That's why they agreed for Aneni to move in with them. Moving to a new place for Aneni was the beginning of a new life, with less worry and pressure.

The new lease of life afforded her the opportunity to enjoy being young without worrying about adult things like school fees. She started well at Mateta 2 Secondary School, even if it was a slight downgrade in terms of quality of education. However, for Aneni, what mattered most was her peace of mind.

As a young girl, who had had exposure to affluent associations at her previous school, she immediately became a new sensation in the new school. She carried on with her refined English accent, which attracted some attention and a bit of gossip by other students. In addition to that, people who lived in teacher's or nurse's quarters were regarded as middle class. Aneni made sure to tell everyone who Madanha and Nevermind were to her family.

"A nurse and a teacher?" she heard someone say. "She's so lucky." Aneni smiled and continued walking, enjoying the new kind of attention she was getting.

Mateta 2 was a semi growth point - it did not have any fancy shops or anything peculiar. The community mainly lived on subsistence farming, and some families had the privilege to venture into cotton farming, which was more rewarding.

The laid back yet vibrant lifestyle fascinated Aneni. In school, she immediately met other young girls who lived in the teacher's cottage. Some of them had had exposure to town life and had a zeal for fashion trends and the latest music. She enjoyed talking to them, and they had quickly become friends. Laughing with her new friends made it easier for Aneni to fit in and forget about her previous school predicaments.

Aneni made a mark at the school during her first English class. The teacher instructed students to write a short essay describing a teacher called Mrs Shiri in the most imaginative way they could. Her short essay read:

Mrs Shiri is a very good teacher. She makes sure that students understand what she teaches. She does not beat students for no apparent reason. She is a genius, and she always looks presentable while ensuring that her dressing is decent and professional. Mrs Shiri is a role model to many. Her commitment to teaching makes her outstanding, and it creates a magnet for students to warm up to her.

It came as a shock that she managed to get nine out of ten for it as she thought that her writing was simple. The teacher made remarks to the whole class, applauding her for being a genius in writing. This boosted her confidence. She wanted to do well. No - she wanted to do better. She finally felt a great sense of purpose without the need to be in a boarding school. From that moment, no matter where she was, that sense of purpose would never leave her.

The news that the new girl had made waves in the English class ran through the school like wildfire, and Aneni felt like a new honour was suddenly bestowed on her. Her new fame had to be a result of the mingling with the affluent who spoke fine English at her previous school. This new fame also meant a lot of interest from people of the opposite sex. Boys would talk about her and to her more and more often. However, Aneni had tried to hold on to mum's advice to finish school first and do boys later.

One afternoon, while Aneni walked home, her heavy bag of books strapped on her shoulder, a young man stopped to talk to her. The young man of medium height, slim and dark in complexion, struck a conversation, complimenting her looks and that he had heard about her English prowess.

"Aneni," he said out each syllable as if his whole life depended on it. "Very unique. Mind telling me why your parents picked it?" The boy, Joe, asked. She could hear just the slightest hint of anxiety and nervousness in his hoarse voice.

"I don't want to talk to you," Aneni responded coldly, showing no interest in having a conversation with him. In those times, it was highly applauded for girls to play uninterested and hard to get.

Joe, however, did not give up. He continued, mentioning that he had known her sister, Mudiwa, when she studied at the same school four years prior. Joe was already a school leaver, waiting to go and work at a nearby cotton company as a farming advisor. In the few days that followed, Joe continued to pursue Aneni and promised her the world. She secretly enjoyed his advances but continued giving him the cold shoulder.

After much thought, as St Valentine's Day was approaching, Aneni thought that she could entertain Joe just so she could get a valentine's gift, and cut the relationship just after the holiday. It was a perfect plan... until it wasn't. Joe continued to be kind and caring, and he even waited for Aneni after school every day. Soon the pretend relationship began to feel more and more real. It felt right to talk to him and laugh with him and call him hers. Love letters began to pour, written in black ink with love hearts all over the paper.

It became a great distraction for her, and each night she would re-read the letters with much enthusiasm, her heart fluttering with each word:

Dear Ane,

You are the most beautiful girl in the world. I cannot live without you, and your voice is a balm to my soul. Sometimes I cannot sleep because I miss you every minute of my life, and when sleep catches me, I see your smile, and the dimples on your face wake me up. I can't wait to see you, my darling.

Yours ever-loving,

Joe.

To Aneni, the relationship seemed more like friendship as there was no touching or intimate kissing. In those days, as young as Aneni was, she had received great counsel from her mum and sisters about the dangers of intimacy before marriage; dangers such as unplanned pregnancy and sexually transmitted infections. But they didn't need intimacy to be happy. Their relationship was as perfect as it could be, and young Aneni found herself thinking about Joe during most of her free time.

Valentine's Day came, and as Aneni expected, she got flowers and a gift - a T-shirt - from Joe. She knew she couldn't tell her sister about Joe as she would then tell her mum, who would be very disappointed in her pre-mature interest in boys. Instead, she talked to a housekeeper who supported the idea of young love. The girl agreed to pretend that the gifts were hers, not Aneni's. This meant that Aneni could look at the beautiful flowers without being scared that someone would find out about Joe.

Her life became dynamic and full of good surprises. She had become closer to her friend, Claudinah. She trusted her so she would talk about Joe and show her the letters from him. Claudinah had also met a boy who was a bit older than her; a boy who worshipped the ground she walked on.

Aneni found herself sitting impatiently in class, waiting for break time, so she could talk about the love she felt and the attention she was getting from Joe. It soon became a part of her routine to walk home from school with Joe. Before Aneni went to bed, she would revise the letters, which made her sleep like a baby, with a smile on her face, and look forward to the day ahead.

The relationship did not deter Aneni from working hard at school. She continued to excel in the English language and public speaking. She also travelled around Gokwe for interschool competitions. Not always did she bring the trophy home, but each time was a learning curve for her. The more exposure she got, the better she became. She also became veritably enthralled by the science subjects as she wanted one day to conquer the mysteries of the universe. As summer was drawing nigh, and the prospects of sitting for the final examinations became real, Aneni created ample time to study, always bearing in mind that her future would be determined by how well she did in school.

All was going well until one early morning, on a Saturday; Joe's mother came to the nurse's quarters on an urgent matter. Aneni opened the door and was perplexed to see her. She immediately greeted her the traditional way of showing respect to elders, half-kneeling while shaking her hands. Joe's mum asked to see her sister Madanha, and she obliged. While they were talking, Aneni kept her ears wide open, fear rising in her chest, wondering if she had found out about her and Joe. Little did she know that her life was about to take a turn for the worse!

"Nurse, forgive me the indecency of not affording you time to rest properly, but I'm here on an emergency. My son's girlfriend came home from Harare. She is eight months pregnant, and she is very unwell."

"Oh, of course. Please, give me five minutes to change into something decent, then we can go," her sister said, but before leaving the room, she stopped. "So, which son is making you a grandma?" she asked. Joe's mum smiled.

"It's my Joe. Didn't he go to school with your other sister?" she said, and Aneni's heart broke into a thousand pieces.

As Aneni's sister Madanha went to change, Aneni collapsed from within. She could not fathom the possibility of Joe lying to her and having a relationship with another woman. She began to ask herself, *why? Why would he do that? Did he not love me? Was I a joke to him, just a distraction, perhaps?*

She started telling herself that the mother must have mentioned the wrong name; that she meant a different son. *Yes, she must have made a mistake with names*, she thought, but deep down, she knew that a mother wouldn't make such a mistake. So, it had to be true: Joe had impregnated another woman. Then great sadness seized her whole being, and she didn't know how to navigate this difficult time. Nothing and nobody had prepared her for this little shipwreck of her life.

The bliss of first love was surely short-lived, and Aneni held back tears day and night. She never thought she would feel so much pain about a boy she wanted to leave after Valentine's Day. The days that followed were full of emotional pain, she would eat less, and her concentration for school was negatively affected. She did not tell her friend immediately as she was filled with shame. The gossip about Joe impregnating a woman ended up spreading through their community like veld fire. Aneni ended the relationship immediately. Joe pleaded with her several times, claiming that he was no longer in love with the other girl. He even went as far as claiming that the baby wasn't his. Aneni told him to stop contacting her. She kept on saying that every time he wrote her a letter or stopped at her school. One time, he finally listened.

Gloomy weather seemed to menacingly hang across Aneni's sky, and it appeared there would surely be no sunshine. An epistle of pain had been engraved profoundly on Aneni's heart and life. Before the incident, Aneni would re-read the love letters that Joe sent her, and this had become her lullaby. Now that the letters made her feel nothing but disgust, she had trouble falling asleep. She had also withdrawn from the activities that usually made her laugh. Finally, after weeks of hiding her sadness, she told her sister exactly what had happened.

"I always advised you against boys, and now look at you," her sister held her in her arms while talking. "You are just a few months away from writing your examinations, and you are just stressing over a boy, and a boy that did not deserve you nonetheless," Madanha said, shaking her head, her tone empathetic. "There are plenty of men in the world that will cherish you. They will do so even more if you have an education. Take this as a lesson and concentrate on your schoolwork."

"Okay, I will focus on studying now."

A wave of silence swept the room. Aneni imagined how her sister might have felt and what she thought of her actions. She felt shame, not only because she had been in a relationship, but also because she had kept it a guarded secret.

Aneni had buried herself in her studies and started spending more time with her friends, even sharing her secrets with them. Some of them were jealous of her short-lived relationship with Joe.

"I would do everything to have a boyfriend like that, even for a minute," one of her friends, Fungai, had told her. "A guy who would pamper me with gifts and love letters and not even ask for anything in return," she swooned at the thought.

"And-," another girl interrupted. "He is good-looking, with a body to die for, and amazing academic skills? A girl can dream, you know?" she flipped her braided hair.

"Maybe Joe was protecting you for marriage, Aneni," said Fungai. "You know most guys nowadays would not just pamper a girl without being intimate with her."

"Well, I am not even ready for marriage, and I want more out of life. I can't imagine having children and tending a home right now. It sounds like a nightmare," Aneni said to her friends in a serious tone. The room fell silent as all the girls contemplated their futures.

"So," Fungai finally said, "what do you want to be after completing o' levels?"

"I think I will look into studying science or teaching, and then further my education. I was thinking about being a university lecturer," Aneni answered. Her friend rolled her eyes to Aneni's high expectations, but she didn't mind. She knew she could do it.

By the time the final Ordinary Level Examinations began, the dust had peacefully settled, and Aneni did not even think about Joe anymore. She continued to study hard so she could pass and follow her dreams. Her passion had always been to succeed in life, get a university degree and help her parents. She did not want to end up in poverty, and she wanted to better her family situation. She had always dreamt of a very comfortable life, characterised by holidays to exotic destinations, a beautiful house in the leafy suburbs of a quiet town, and perhaps a swimming pool, and a good car. She understood that all her dreams could only come true through hard work. So, she worked hard. She worked hard in school and stayed open to other avenues that could present her with better opportunities in life. But no matter what she did, she always kept her dream alive; doing everything she could to make it a reality.

The examinations were soon behind her, and her journey at Mateta 2 soon became a closed chapter; a chapter- if possible- she would rather it remained closed forever. She painfully bid farewell to her friends, who had made her life in Gokwe full of fun and worth remembering. There were tears of sadness and promises to meet again.

At the last assembly, the head teacher made a speech.

"You must be feeling excited to leave school, to explore the world. I tell you, the years you spend at school are, and always will be, the happiest. The world is full of uncertainties. It is waiting to devour you at every opportunity it gets, and it does not forgive. Embrace change, and do not let the world devour you. Keep working hard, as hard as you can. Some of you will die earlier than others. Some of you will get the privilege of getting old enough to meet your grandchildren. Make wise decisions today and not tomorrow. Fare thee well."

Chapter 4

After bidding farewell to friends and acquaintances, Aneni packed her bags and went back home to mum and dad. She had not seen them in a long time. The longing was killing her, which made the long bus ride even more unbearable. She allowed herself to bath in the peace and quiet of the days after the examination period. If someone had asked her, "What do you want to do now, Aneni?" she would have answered without hesitation, "To float like a cloud." She did not want to worry; she simply wanted to be close to her parents after such a long time.

Aneni relished the love that mum and dad gave her the time she returned home. She was not the youngest, but there were no other children at home except her at that time. She would go to church with mum and spend time at home with her parents doing farm work and relaxing. They enjoyed their evening tea, a family tradition where they would spend time chatting in the evening over a cup of tea. Sometimes the tea had milk, sometimes it did not. It made no difference. They even sat down to drink tea during the hottest weather, keeping the tradition alive. Her parents told her that the tradition was adopted from the English, but it was so long ago they had now considered it their own.

During the discussions that Aneni had with her mum, she often heard the argument of *no intimacy before marriage*. She made sure to highlight that the purer the woman was, the more respected she would be by her spouse. This was also a cultural and societal expectation: girls should preserve themselves for marriage because that attracted honourable husbands. The expectations for boys were different. No one expected a boy to get married as a virgin, or even if they were, nobody cared because it did not make much of a difference. It did not make them lesser men.

Aneni listened to her mother and valued not being intimate until marriage. She wanted to keep herself pure, not just to receive honour from her husband, but also for herself; to lessen the possibility of unwanted pregnancies and sexually transmitted infections. Aneni noticed the disparity between what was expected of young girls, and what was- or was not- expected of boys, and felt that it perpetuated unfair treatment based on gender. She didn't think, though, that any platform for her voice to be heard concerning this issue could be found, so she just kept quiet. She did, however, make a mental note of all the unfair stereotypes regarding young girls and decided to fight against it. While she would find herself in relationships with men, she made sure her principles and values were laid out at the beginning of the relationship. She also made sure that there would be no compromise when it came to her morals and values. She made sure that she was comfortable, and that the boundaries were kept.

Aneni did not have much of a social life besides staying at home and going to church on Sundays. She became introverted as she enjoyed relaxing at home rather than interacting with other girls from the village. There was no boyfriend in the picture either. She focused her energy on the farm and house chores, fetching firewood, getting water from the local borehole, pounding maize to make samp, and weeding the fields with her parents. She did not mind a bit of solitude in her free time.

At the farm, there was a mango orchard, which bore a variety of juicy mangoes. Being Aneni's favourite fruit, she enjoyed having mangoes for breakfast and lunch.

Sometimes she and MaMushambi would sell the mangoes to the local market vendors. The time passed slowly as she waited for her Ordinary Level results, so she sat in the shade of the trees and learnt not to mind.

Her main motivation to always work hard was the product of her immense desire to improve her parents' lives. This was triggered by several different issues. However, there was one incident that made her feel the urgency to take a step towards her plan.

Aneni preferred to sleep in the living room on the couch because it was close to her parents' bedroom. She did not feel very comfortable sleeping in the girls' quarters as it made her feel lonely without her sisters.

The rains in mid-January of 1999 were incessant and it rained non-stop which made it difficult for farmers to go and work in the fields. Most families stayed indoors and only went out to do necessary chores. Some crops did not sprout as expected because of too much water. Farmers were on edge. There were fears that the year would go to waste. This would be a different kind of hunger. People were used to understanding hunger and famine to be caused by drought- a lack of rain- and not the other way round. Aneni's parents would wake up in the morning and draw the curtain to their bedroom to see if the rain had subsided, but it stubbornly did not stop.

On one of the many rainy nights, while Aneni was asleep, she heard a knock coming from her parents' bedroom.

"Who is that?" she asked in a sleepy voice.

"It's me," MaMushambi said. "Can you move the couch you're sleeping on a little? It's raining non-stop, and the crack on the ceiling may get worse. I don't want it to fall on you." Aneni pushed the sofa that she slept on to the other side of the room.

As she was going back to sleep, she stared at the crack and felt so much pain in her heart, thinking how her parents had lived for so long in a house that was not safe. Although she could not do anything to better the situation at the time, she felt compelled to work hard to ensure that one day, she would renovate her parents' home. This way they could live without fear of the house crumbling down while they were sleeping.

Soon after Christmas, the Ordinary Level examination results came out. The suspense was immense for Aneni as she waited impatiently for her sister Madanha to send the results to her. At that time, there were no phones, so there was no way her sister could tell her about the results except through registered mail.

Five days later, the results came, and Aneni immediately opened the mail with her trembling hands.

"Yes, I have passed! Mummy, I passed!" Aneni's grades were good enough to get a head start on her new future as an adult.

As they say, the journey of a thousand miles begins with a single step. Aneni had to sit down and decide which way she wanted her life to go. In her mind, she had determined to better her parents' life and to eventually relocate to a First World country. She didn't know why, but she always felt connected to England and decided that she wanted to move there. She was sure she could get out of poverty, and early marriage was not in her plans. As the days went on, it became evident that there would be no fees for Aneni to proceed to the Advanced Level. So, she was content with the dream to go abroad and work hard.

At the time, Zimbabwe was going through the land reform programme, which attracted sanctions from the West. The local currency was losing its once great value, with inflation rates skyrocketing by the minute. Salaries remained stagnant, while prices of commodities were going up to an all-time high.

People would go into a shop to buy an item at one price, only to return a few minutes later with the price highly inflated. The situation was getting worse each day. The people were panicking about how they were to sustain their families. A great wave of citizens began to relocate to neighbouring countries and overseas in search of greener pastures. Many of Aneni's schoolmates at Biriiri High School had relocated to the United Kingdom and some to the United States and Australia. Others had moved to neighbouring countries such as South Africa, Namibia and Mozambique.

At the time, it was difficult for Aneni to think of relocating because she simply did not have the financial resources to do so. However, she was not comfortable staying at home and hoped to get a teaching or nursing post in the near future. She had tried to apply for so long, but the demand was too high and getting a place at the time required one to know someone in the system.

She became a friend of the regional newspaper, The Manica Post, which her dad usually brought from his social interactions. She would peruse the vacancies section to see if she could get a part-time job. However, all she could get were domestic work jobs. She would quickly go past the domestic work posts as she had no interest in becoming a house help.

She kept looking for weeks until it dawned on her that it was an exercise in futility. She was tired. One day, she sat down to have evening tea with her mum and looked at her.

"Mum, I was thinking," she started, raising the cup to her lips. "I could temporarily work as a house help rather than sit at home. To make some money before I find a better job." In her family, no one had ever been a housemaid before. She didn't want to do it, but she thought that her dream was too big, and she needed a place to start. MaMushambi was a bit uneasy about it.

"Well, it can keep you busy while you prepare for better things," she said. It made sense, and Aneni started looking at the domestic help section of Manica Post. *Just for now*, she told herself, always dreaming big.

Chapter 5

"We only have one young child to take care of. He is very independent so your job will be to make sure he does things on time," Mai Mutya said while giving Aneni an ample briefing before she could start the job. The family seemed fine and easy to live with. Aneni was happy to be doing something productive rather than staying at home, hoping that the future would mend itself.

Aneni packed her bag. It was not a fancy bag, but it served its purpose effectively. She did not have a lot of clothes either, so it was easy to pack. She hoped that one day she would buy any type of clothes she wanted with her own money, but for now, she had to be happy with what she had.

The Mutya family lived a bit outside of the local town Mutare on a beautiful plot in Penhalonga. They were religious people and frequented one of the most prominent Pentecostal churches, Forward in Faith. They had three grown-up girls, one at university, and the other two at boarding schools. They also had two young sons, one of them lived away with Mrs Mutya's sister and the last born, Nyasha, was the only child living with them at home. He was seven years old.

After Aneni arrived at their home, she was immediately shown to her cosy bedroom, with good quality linen sheets. This was her room, and she would not have to share it with anyone else. Mrs Mutya showed her the rest of the house, and all the rooms exuded comfort and luxury.

The Mutya family sat her down and laid out in detail what needed to be done, and they agreed to pay her 700 Zimbabwean dollars. It was not much, but it was enough for Aneni to set sail on her journey towards a brighter future.

According to their arrangement, she could go home on some weekends, leaving on Friday afternoon and returning on Sundays. This sounded like a good deal, and it put a smile on her face.

Aneni was not new to doing house chores, although she had to learn a few modern ways of cleaning as the house setup was different from the house she was used to cleaning. She was consistent in her work, waking up early to get Nyasha ready for school, make porridge and prepare his lunch. When Mr Mutya and Nyasha had left, she would then do laundry and clean the house and do a bit of gardening.

She would go home some weekends and stay at work on other weekends. She usually went home on the weekends that she received her pay so she could buy a few groceries for her parents.

Six months passed, and Aneni felt that her life had come to a halt. The salary she was getting was not going to be enough to fulfil her dreams of studying in the United Kingdom and rebuilding her parents' home. She needed to restrategise.

Aneni had started to conceive the idea of moving to Mozambique in search of a temporary job to sponsor her dream. She started to imagine, ponder and fantasise about how she was going to make her way to Mozambique, and all her dreams would come true. She did not know anyone who lived there and could help her move. Neither did she earn enough to afford accommodation and food while awaiting job opportunities. She thought about the dangers she could face as a young girl, taking on such an uncertain and possibly dangerous adventure. She pondered where she would be accommodated and how she would find a job.

Where could she start looking for a job without a passport and proper documents that would enable her to work in a foreign country? Aneni was not oblivious of all the challenges and dangers that could be lying ahead. This, however, did not deter her to dream, thinking that going to Mozambique was her only way out of poverty and gateway to sponsoring her to go to the United Kingdom. So broad was the will, but so narrow the means.

Aneni continued to work diligently, which won the hearts of her employers. Besides the diligent work, Mrs Mutya had commented that Aneni was a very well-behaved young girl who set a good example to her children. They would give her clothes they no longer needed and groceries when she was going home. She had cared for Mr Mutya's ailing mother when she had come to stay with them temporarily after being discharged from hospital due to a heart and foot swelling condition. She had shared the room with her, swapping her place on the cosy bed for the cold, uninviting floor. Every morning before she started working, she would make sure that grandma had porridge so that she could take her medication. Throughout the day, she would take particular care in what grandma wanted to eat as she did not always have an appetite for certain foods. She would always make sure her laundry was done and that she was happy. This did not go unnoticed; The Mutya extended family members were enchanted when they came to visit. It was apparent that each day she passed a little test- the little tests which would however become valuable later in life.

Eight months passed, and life fell into a monotonous routine as nothing new or exciting was happening in Aneni's life. Despite the contentment in her work, she yearned for a new challenge, a new chapter. In this new chapter, she wanted her dream to be fulfilled. She envisioned greatness, but she also acknowledged that greatness was not going to be easy. She understood that tears and fears were likely to be part of that journey to greatness. The depth and extent of the tears and fears she was not privy to. In her mind, she expected challenges but probably only the simple, normal challenges that every human being comes across at some point in their life. She believed her demeanour, principles, and hard work would make her happy. Not only that, but also that the love and trust that her parents had invested in her would keep her focused and grounded.

One evening, while coming back from her off-weekend, Aneni eavesdropped on two ladies who talked about border jumping. The ladies sounded like cross-border traders who used the clandestine ways to cross into Mozambique with clothes and shoes for sale. In the conversation, they had also mentioned that some people were earning United States dollars as English teachers in Mozambique.

Mozambique was once a Portuguese colony, and the locals spoke Portuguese and other vernacular languages. Therefore, due to more influx in trade and interaction with English speaking neighbouring countries, there was a need for some Mozambicans to want to learn to speak English. This particular eavesdropping had then expanded the array of money-raising possibilities towards her dream. Raising money for a passport would seemingly further delay the whole process. Moreover, at that time, getting a passport was not easy; therefore border jumping was quicker and more plausible. Aneni tried to put the thoughts away, but they kept coming back, making her dream seem closer if she only took a chance.

One sunny morning, Aneni's employers and children had all gone out. They had told her that they would return the next day, so she needed not to prepare food for anyone but herself. It became an unofficial off-day for Aneni, as she had the whole house to herself and did not need to do much for anyone. On this day, she did her housework as diligently as usual. After doing the last bits of her work, she thought she could visit the local shopping centre and treat herself to some eet-sum-mor, her favourite biscuits. In the same thought, she saw an opportunity to find more information about the clandestine border jumping into Mozambique. She did not know anyone who could provide that information. However, as with any bustling place, the market was a source of valuable local information. In most places, markets and beauty salons were the source of current affairs of any locality. Unexploited media houses!

She arrived at the shopping centre and approached the women who were seated at the market. Most of them were selling fruit and vegetable produce; tomatoes, onions, and avocados. In her opinion, it wasn't proper to seek valuable information without buying any of their products. She gathered a few coins from her worn-out purse, and as she approached the young women, a wave of uncertainty and apprehension overwhelmed her. She thought to herself, *what if they can't offer her any help in fear of being caught in the syndicate of breaking immigration rules? What if they sell me out to the police? Or worse: what if they don't have any information at all?* She forced herself to calm down and put a smile on her face. After all, uncertainty and fear had never helped her achieve any goals. She approached the lovely ladies, ignoring the fear and letting hope take over her words. The lady smiled at her. *Bingo!*

The days that followed the visit to the market were hectic, filled with hope, excitement and immense fear of the unknown. Aneni gathered the courage to sit down and tell her employers that she was going to look for a place to train as a teacher. She could not dare to think of telling them the truth of where she was going. As painful as it was to leave such a loving and warm family, life had to happen, and she had to follow her dreams. She gave in four weeks' notice to the family, to their obvious dismay. However, they gave her their blessings, thanked her for being an exemplary house help, and wished her well.

In the four weeks that followed, she immersed herself in critical planning of the trip: how much money would she need? How many pieces of clothes could she carry given that the journey was to be mainly undertaken on foot? What bags and belongings will she take? What will she tell her parents?

She decided that she could not keep such a big secret from them. She was honest and told her parents that she was going to look for greener pastures in Mozambique, with the hope that it would finance her way to the United Kingdom. She told them that she would keep in touch and keep them updated. From the savings she had gathered, she gave her parents some money for basics.

"You are very strong and courageous. God will keep you safe," MaMushambi said and wrapped her arms around her daughter. As she boarded the bus, her mother's words rang loudly in her ears, filling her with confidence.

Chapter 6

In July of 2001, a dark cloud hung menacingly across the sky, but the birds sang as if they were singing for her. It was nearly the end of the Zimbabwe winter, transitioning into spring. However, the breeze could still cause discomfort to walk about without some layers on. The mood and ambience of the general environment were serene. The trees shook no longer, only the scarce drop of dry leaves could be heard here and there. There was no pressure, and the trees still looked beautiful in their shedding season. Everything seemed beautiful and calm. Within, Aneni was a mess. She was the perfect embodiment of- as absurd as it may sound-hollowness, fear, courage, passion for fulfilment and more. Aneni knew that, to achieve the colourful dreams of her future, she had to survive an arduous and terrifying journey.

She felt the nod of power as if the knowledge that she was starting over, her life a blank page, made her more confident that it needed to be done. The uncertainty made life more poetic for Aneni, who looked forward to the fragile future with a confident smile. She didn't realise that her hope made her constantly brush aside the grave challenges that could be lying ahead for her.

The boat was about to set sail. The beginning of a new dream was being born; a new era.

Aneni had packed her bags the night before. She had opted for a rucksack and a very small bag with a stretchable handle. The rucksack had seen better days. She had inherited it from her older brother, Maguza. It was made out of very durable material, but had apparently seen better days.

In the rucksack, she packed a few clothes and left some space to put a few things to eat for the journey. The rest of her clothes, shoes and other supplies perfectly fitted in her small bag.

Aneni had practised the night before how she would carry the bags so that the weight would be less uncomfortable. She thought to herself, *there is no more turning back. This is it!*

The Mutya family had prayed with her, and she thanked them for allowing her to work and learn new skills in life. Mr Mutya had offered to drive with her to the town, where she could take a bus to her destination.

"I will be setting off later than you," she said, trying to hide her lies. She couldn't tell him that she wasn't planning on taking the bus to Mutare, but was actually planning to cross the mountains in Penhalonga to get to Mozambique. If she accepted his offer, she would go in the opposite direction to where she needed to be, but she couldn't tell that to him without revealing her real plans.

Aneni was ready to leave the Mutya home at ten in the morning, and surprisingly, the weather had slightly changed as the sun was out and shining. With the love for nature that besotted Aneni, the weather was quite an inspiration for her. It made her feel like it was a sign that everything would go as planned. On the day of the journey, Aneni wore a simple black skirt as she did not wear trousers a lot. Wearing trousers as a girl gave the impression that the girl was somehow loose and liked boys. That was, of course, not the case, but rather an ignorant community stereotype that put people in a certain bracket based on their choice of clothes, hair, music or lifestyle. She matched the skirt with a white spaghetti top and an unbuttoned check shirt on top.

On her feet, she put on simple black pumps, which would sustain her throughout the journey.

Mrs Mutya offered to walk her to the bus stop. Aneni could not turn down that offer as that would seem rude and unappreciative. She conceded, and Mrs Mutya escorted her to the bus stop where she could get transport to Mutare even though she was really going in the opposite direction. Aneni thought to herself, *I will play the part and figure out ways to return.*

"Oh, that's a nice ride and very comfortable," Mrs Mutya said when they got to the bus stop. She hugged Aneni and waved goodbye as she got into the back seat of the double cabin Toyota Hilux vehicle. Aneni waved at Mrs Mutya from the window, and she waved back with a smile.

The driver was quite engaging. He tried to start a conversation asking Aneni about her life, school and where she came from. Aneni was responding to the driver while mindfully plotting a way to get out of the vehicle before it went too far. She was not paying much attention to what the driver was saying; only responding with one-word answers. After about four kilometres it was time to put her plan in motion.

"Oh my God," Aneni gasped, "I left something very important at home." The driver was full of concern. He slowed down and asked what she would want to do. "Can you please drop me here? I can get a lift back home to collect it," she said. The driver nodded.

"Of course. I am sorry, young lady. I hope you will be able to get to where you are going on time," he added.

"Yes, I will. Don't worry," she said kindly. The driver stopped and kindly waited for Aneni to catch a lift that would take her back to where he had picked her. After a couple of minutes, a Santana Land Cruiser- a police patrol vehicle- stopped and gave Aneni a lift back to Penhalonga.

She got to Penhalonga shopping centre and went straight to the local supermarket. She picked out six sugar buns, a pack of sliced polony, three small bottles of cascade orange flavoured drink, as well as some sweets and crisps. She also bought two bottles of water, hoping that all this would sustain her on the trip.

She immediately packed her food in the rucksack, put the rucksack behind her, and strapped the small bag on her shoulder. The journey had begun. At nineteen, she was ready to face the mountain that awaited her. Beyond that mountain lay the hope of finally achieving her dreams.

Penhalonga is a valley surrounded by a vast mountainous terrain. In Portuguese, *Penha* means *rocky mountain*, while *Longa* means *long*. The name is a perfect representation of the area. The mountain she was going to walk through towards the Mozambican border was one of the highest in the area, which is why it was strategically marked as the border, to discourage people from crossing it. The mountain was not only high and long, but it was also very dense. There were so many different types of trees, almost the level of a rainforest, which made the trails narrow and hard to walk through.

As she headed upwards towards the trail, Penhalonga town now behind her, Aneni turned and looked back. There were tears in her eyes.

"My beloved country, I love you, but for now, I am leaving you. See you soon," she said before turning around. The journey had started, and she followed the advice she had been given by the market ladies. She did not want to raise any alarm by bidding them farewell before leaving, lest they notify the police, not because of malice, but simply because they could have felt that Aneni was too young to take on such a risky journey by herself.

For an hour, Aneni walked without any problems. The day was quite peaceful, and it did not appear as if there was anyone else crossing the border that day. She had expected to at least see a few people walking the same route, but there was no one else there. However, she remembered the market ladies saying most cross-border traders cross the border very early in the morning. This was convenient for them as they would sell their merchandise and probably return on the same day late afternoon. It made sense, and for Aneni, the agenda was a parallel one.

The peace and quiet of the afternoon was occasionally interrupted by loud chirps from the honey birds, as if they were cheering her on. She walked boldly; a kind of boldness that was normally coupled with fear. The forest was quite dense, such that when she had walked for an hour, she stopped to look back from where she had come from, and all she could see was the vast expanse of forest. She reassured herself that she was alright and would reach her destination in one piece. As noon approached, the temperatures were getting warmer. Sweat poured on Aneni's skin as she walked. She took off the checked shirt and tied it around her slim waist. She also rearranged her bags for more comfort as the climb was becoming more tiring. She continued to walk with determination. After all, beyond the simple advice to *follow the trail*, she had no idea where she was going and how long it would take to cross into Mozambique.

In her mind, Aneni was at acquired peace- peace that she deliberately chose so that she would not get tired too quickly. She made sure to think positive thoughts like her love for adventure, her time at school, her friends and her family. She wondered where most of her friends would be by the time she accomplished her goals. She also thought about herself returning home with wealth, enough wealth to rebuild her parents' home, and how happy that would make them. As she thought of home, she found herself humming her favourite church hymn, *Mwari Mubatsiri Wangu*. This hymn represented God as the centre of one's life, the guide, author and finisher of one's faith. It made sense for Aneni to carry that hymn in her heart. The song was more of a United Methodist church anthem as it was sung a lot at events and church conferences. It reminded her of home and her community.

As she approached the Peak of Penhalonga Mountain, Aneni heard some squashing noise, the sound of something or rather someone walking in the woods. Her heart skipped a bit. The dense forest did not allow her to see far beyond where she stood. The sound continued, each time sounding closer and closer. She did not know whether to hide or not. Cautiously, she trekked on, slower than she had been doing. Her heart continued to sink with fear. Her legs were getting weak of anxiety, sweat gushing from her brow.

As the noise became more pronounced, a young man appeared, possibly in his early twenties. He wore a blue T-shirt and black shorts and had nothing in his hands. He was walking fast, and as he approached, Aneni gave way for him to pass. The young man did not greet Aneni as he hurried past. Meanwhile, Aneni's heart was drumming as she struggled to gather herself together. Fear gripped her as she thought to herself, *what if he runs back and rapes me or kills me?*

She let a few tear drops roll down her cheeks while walking with more urgency than before. After about thirty minutes of brisk walking with no further incident, she let out a sigh of relief.

As she neared the peak of the mountain, now extremely tired, she noticed there was a tent erected a few yards from where she was. She wondered what the tent was for, and as she approached, she deliberately walked slowly so as not to alarm anyone who could've been inside. Aneni was not privy to the whole procedure of clandestine border jumping, and the market ladies only had a rough idea of how the process was done, but they did not mention anything about a tent. They had just told her to find the trail and she thought that was all that mattered.

As she slowly passed the tent, she heard a male voice. Aneni turned her head to see who it was, perplexed to see a stout male holding a gun which looked like an AK 47. She had learnt about the AK 47 from the history books as the most used rifle in the Zimbabwe's second Chimurenga war. The man pointed the weapon right at her. She could feel tears running down her face as she stared at the barrel of a gun for the first time in her life. Her knees felt weak, and she fell to the ground.

All forms of energy in her body instantly left her, and the bag that she had on her shoulder was now rolling slowly down the trail in the dirt. Sweat gushed from her face, and she wondered for a second where that much sweat was coming from.

Oh, my parents. Am I dying here without doing anything of what I promised you? Aneni thought to herself. It appeared surreal, and it was happening all so fast. The adventure that she had set herself on was a stupid dream. She would die here, with no one around, her body never to be found. She let out a sob, feeling her dreams and life fleeting away.

In that rush of thought, Aneni heard the man speak, in a language quite similar to Shona, her mother-tongue, but not quite the same. It then took time for her to comprehend what he was saying. She swallowed her tears and gathered the courage to get up and look at the man.

"Good afternoon, sir. Sorry, I didn't notice that there was someone here," Aneni said in very well-polished English, with a thick British accent. For some strange reason, Aneni's fear subsided when she opened her mouth to speak. The man looked at her.

"Me, no English," he grunted.

"What language do you speak?"

"Little bit Shona."

"Okay," she responded. This time, the man had become suddenly soft and quite concerned. He stopped pointing the gun at her.

"Are you by yourself on this dangerous trail? Where are you going?" he asked in broken Shona. Questions kept pouring, and eventually, Aneni answered in Shona, saying that she was going to Mozambique to look for an English teaching job. The man's face immediately registered great concern. "I know how difficult life in Zimbabwe currently is, and it's sad to see young women like you risking their lives for a better future."

Aneni was surprised at the quick turn of events. She still felt immense fear. She was alone with a strange man in, what appeared to be, a very secluded place, with no one in sight and no houses or buildings nearby. Just because the man turned nice to her, it did not mean she wasn't in danger.

The man continued, saying that he was a Guarda Frontera, which meant border security guard. And he said that everyone had to report themselves at his post even without travel documents. The Guarda Frontera was there to ensure that no contraband or dangerous weapons were being smuggled into their country. In practical terms, it was an informal border patrol post.

Courteously, the Guarda Frontera laid down his AK47 on the roadside, taking great caution not to pull the trigger.

"Here, you can take your bag," the Guarda Frontera said after he carefully picked and dusted off her bag.

"Thank you very much," she mumbled in a faint but relieved tone. The Guarda Frontera advised Aneni which trail to take and assured her that she had not long until she would get to the main road. From there it would be a short journey to the nearest town.

Aneni had learnt early on that the power dynamics always presented themselves in more ways than one. She knew that having more money than others meant power; that being more intelligent meant power; being a man meant power. At this moment, she felt how much power the Guarda Frontera had over people who dared to cross the border clandestinely. Instantly, she realised the power that a young, soft-spoken woman could have, getting what she desired by picking the right tone of voice.

The sigh of relief made Aneni feel like herself again. She had been paralysed by fear since she had met the young man on the trail. Now, as she smiled and walked away from Guarda Frontera, she felt light and confident, sure that the hardest part was behind her. The guard's words rang in her ears: *it's sad to see young women like you risking their lives for a better future.*

Weird, she thought to herself, *I do not consider myself young.* Aneni thought that people were only as young or as old as they let their minds and hearts be. She felt herself, she felt whole and she felt mature. She felt confident enough to navigate her own life in an effort to achieve her dreams. She did not want pity from a stranger. Life was already overflowing with pity, and she was too strong to drown in it.

Chapter 7

The descent from Mount Penhalonga to the main road was less painful than the climb up. After the encounter with the Guarda Frontera, Aneni was now trekking on Mozambican land. It felt surreal but fulfilling: the bridge to her promised land; the catalyst to the brighter future that lay patiently ahead. *Not too bad after all,* she thought as she approached the main dusty road.

The beautiful yellow sun was almost setting when Aneni got to the main road. She wondered if she would get any transport at that hour. The place was deserted. The silence and tranquillity of the village of Vanduzi area filled her with apprehension. She was not too naïve to understand that seeing no one around could mean she was not safe. But for now, she felt a simmer of pride- a sense of accomplishment as she had managed to conquer what was so far the most difficult task of her life- cross from Zimbabwe into Mozambique, alone, on foot.

Aneni had not eaten since the beginning of her trip as she wanted to save her resources in case she got lost. Anxiety and nervousness somehow had the power to eradicate any form of hunger and eating. At this point, eating was a matter of principle to nourish her body to survive the unknown that beckoned ahead. She knew that she had to eat something so that she could retain energy and continue her travels. She opened her rucksack and took out some sugar buns and an orange cascade drink to accompany the meal. The food that once tasted divine seemed tasteless, but she made sure to finish it all. She stood at the crossroads, more hopeful for the future, but she was also frightened as she did not know where her life was going. She didn't even know where she was going to sleep that night and whether she would be able to sleep without fearing for her life.

Aneni loved nature. She always did. She was fascinated by the sunrise, the sunset, the moon, the stars, mountains, lakes, farms, deserts and the melodious music from the birds. It made her feel happy and peaceful - it made her feel alive. Her insatiable love for nature was caused by her upbringing at the farm. The farm was surrounded by mountains and vast forests. Paying tribute to mother Earth and admiring her gifts became an everyday ritual for her.

As she sat on the ground in an unfamiliar land, she felt reassurance while looking at the familiar sun. The faint rays of dusk made her worried about her sleeping situation, but it did not stop her from admiring the beauty of the colourful sky. As she stared at the disappearing sun, she continued to hope that an opportunity would soon present itself; that divine providence would take care of things.

She soon decided to get up, walk around and see if she could find any traces of people who could help her seek with a place to put up for the night.

Aneni had just walked for a couple of minutes when suddenly she saw a cloud of dust in the distance. She stopped immediately and let herself hope that something, maybe a car was causing the dust. She stared at the far away disruption of peace and, suddenly, there it was - a noise. A car.

She tried to wave it down, but the dust was covering her vision, and she wasn't sure if the driver would see her. Suddenly, she feared that the car would not stop because she too was covered in dusty mist, which made her invisible.

The car approached, and Aneni continued to wave with more vigour and urgency. To her dismay, the car passed Aneni, and she started to weep in her heart. Her only hope was lost.

In her helplessness, she continued to wave even after the truck had passed her. To her surprise, the truck reduced speed and stopped a few yards from where she stood. Aneni couldn't believe her eyes, and for a moment, she just stood there, not knowing what to do. She took off, running towards the vehicle, clutching her possessions tightly against her body.

Aneni reached the truck, her breathing heavy, her voice trembling as she approached the driver's window to ask for a lift.

"I have just got here, and I am looking for a lift to Manica town. Is that where you are going?" she asked the driver in Shona. At this time, Aneni would have just pushed herself into the truck whether it was headed to her destination or not. The driver looked at her from head to toe, perhaps wondering what such a young girl, covered in dust, was doing so late in the middle of nowhere. Finally, he looked her in the eyes.

"Yes, I'm driving to Manica," he said in a dry tone with a broken Shona accent. The district of Manica was closest to the Zimbabwean border, and most people in the district spoke Portuguese and Sena. Sena is quite similar to Shona but spoken with a distinct accent. Aneni couldn't help but thank God for her luck. The driver said that if she wanted a ride, she would have to pay twenty meticals, the Mozambican currency. She agreed.

The vehicle was an open truck, and the passenger seat was already occupied, which meant that she would have to sit in the back. She threw her bag in the back and jumped in. The truck started moving almost immediately.

She wasn't alone at the back. Two other ladies, each sitting on a big bag of rice, were sitting next to her. Aneni noticed that one of them was carrying a child on her back.

"Como Estas?" one of the ladies said in Portuguese. Aneni assumed that it was a greeting, although she did not quite understand what it meant. She also didn't know how to respond.

"Hello. Nice to meet you," she mumbled with a confused tone as she did not know if the ladies knew any English, and she didn't want to act like a snob, showing off her English abilities. In moments of vulnerability, snobbish behaviour does not come in handy at all.

Aneni decided to strike up a conversation with the ladies. She started by asking, "Do you understand Shona?" The ladies looked at each other and said they understood but spoke just a little. One of the ladies was a *mulata*, which in Portuguese meant *a person of mixed race*. The other lady was black, like Aneni.

"I'm Gina, and this is Mara," the black woman said. "Are you going to Manica?" Aneni couldn't imagine all the questions that the ladies could have of her, a young, pretty girl who stood in the middle of nowhere so late.

"I'm Aneni. And yes, I am," she replied.

"Oh, so are you going there for business, or are you visiting relatives?" Gina asked.

"I am going to look for an English teaching job... or any other job. I want to raise money to fly to the United Kingdom and study there," she explained. The ladies exchanged looks. "Do you know any places where I can find a room to rent? I don't know anyone in Manica," she added. The ladies looked at each other again.

"It is not possible to find a place to rent at this time," Mara said, shaking her head. "You don't know anyone there? You came without a plan?" Similar questions kept coming, and as truthful and appropriate as they were, they pricked right through Aneni's heart as she realised that the reality of her new life had just begun. She immediately felt destitute, and the treatment thereof of a destitute from others was inevitable. Aneni did not, however, want to take offence at the harsh response from Mara and her constant questions. She felt that Mara had every right to be alarmed by such an adventurous young lady.

She continued to feel the need to act humble, the way MaMushambi had taught her. Humbleness can take you far in life. In a coy, soft voice she said, "No, I do not know anyone. I have nowhere to sleep today. I don't know what I will do."

There was silence for a significant length of time as the two women looked at each other. Everyone must have been wondering how to proceed after being faced with such a challenge. What should Aneni do?

"You are a very young woman," Mara said. "Some people will want to take advantage of you. They will steal from you, rape you."

"I understand that. If I had arrived early, I would have sought accommodation in daylight. But unfortunately, I had trouble with my transport, and now here I am," Aneni said, with a humbled voice, looking at the dark night sky.

"Well, you can come and sleep at my house for tonight, but you have to promise you are not a kidnapper. I have children!" Mara said, with slight hesitation, but Aneni could see that her heart was full of compassion.

"Oh, thank you," she stopped, tears pooling in her eyes. "Thank you so very much. You can trust me, I am harmless, I promise!" she quickly added. Aneni felt an insurmountable relief within her. She couldn't even imagine how difficult it would be for her to find any form of accommodation in a foreign land with no acquaintances or family.

She analysed Mara's demeanour and convinced herself that she did not appear like the type that would harm her. One, because she had a baby with her, and secondly, she looked like a simple person who tried to make ends meet in an honest way. Aneni wondered about the kind of accommodation that Mara had and whether it bore some comfort. She immediately dismissed the thought upon realising that she was at a point of desperation and had no choice. Therefore, she prepared herself for any kind of lifestyle which lay ahead. She would be grateful no matter what conditions she would face.

The rest of the journey became more relaxed for Aneni, as she knew she would have a bed for a night. She stared at the starry night sky and breathed in deeply. She didn't dare to think about tomorrow, as she thought tomorrow would sort itself, just as that day had sorted itself.

On the final leg of the journey, Aneni asked what Mara and Gina were doing that made them travel so late.

"Things are hard here. There are no jobs, especially for us. We are not educated enough," Gina said. "Most of us, including Mara and I, have resorted to more... informal business," she pointed at the bag of rice she was sitting on.

"We buy big sacks of rice and resell it in small portions in the nearby villages. It is hard work, but we are managing."

"It is always amazing to see women work very hard to keep their families afloat," Aneni commented. Gina nodded and mentioned that they were making a stable living from buying and reselling rice. It was enough to cater for the needs of the family. There was a clear sense of pride in her voice.

Aneni hesitated to prompt whether the ladies were married or had partners who were helping them. But from her brief observations and some comments they had made, she concluded that they were strong single women running families by themselves. Aneni came from a school of thought of independence in women. She never understood women being too dependent on men, as she had witnessed many women falling at the mercy of men who provided for them. She had heard stories of women staying in abusive marriages simply because they had no means and resources to fend for themselves and their children. She pondered how unfair it was to expect women to never earn their own and fall at the mercy of their husbands. What would happen if the husband, the only provider, died? Or left his family for one reason or another? With minimal to no education and no work experience, those women's lives would fall apart.

Aneni concluded in her thoughts that, even if a woman is married and is well provided for by the husband, she should always know how to create income and how to run a family effectively. This did not only benefit the family, but the sanity and contentment of the woman.

Aneni thought of herself as an independent woman. She had taken it upon herself to go out there and scrap for opportunities when she could easily find a man to get married to. If she did that, she wouldn't have to worry about her welfare. However, Aneni valued hard work, and marriage to her was not the ultimate goal in life. She wanted more. She wanted to go out there and experience the world, enrich herself and become a force to be reckoned with. She wanted to travel, to study, to live. Aneni dreamt of getting married one day, but she did not want to enter into marriage empty - she wanted to be a fully formed person, with opinions and experiences of her own- before she could commit to being with someone for a lifetime. It mattered to her that her future husband would cherish her aspirations and would not be intimidated by her desire to achieve more.

Aneni looked at Gina and Mara, and she realised that they appeared very content with their lives. She guessed that the feeling of managing to put food on the table for their families was enough - they did not bother much about other extravagant ambitions. It could also have been circumstances that made them conform to a simple life, circumstances that made them not gain any opportunities outside of their current situation. Aneni thought there must be an array of mindsets in the world where some people are pushed by meagre circumstances into doing bigger and better things while others remained in the comfort of that meagreness without feeling the need or pressure to change the status quo.

She was amazed that Gina and Mara were working hard for their families, but she thought to herself that she would not be content to stay meagre.

As Aneni was engaging with the ladies, she immediately felt at home with them. But she wanted far more than to be content with buying and reselling rice to afford food on the table. She thought to herself, *I want more.*

I want to be able to have enough to help others; to travel the world and live as comfortably as possible. As this was going through her mind, she also acknowledged how different aspirations and ambitions were. The dynamic of class and ambition was necessary to bring a balance in society. She felt that a well-off person would have never offered her a place to sleep because they would not trust strangers around their riches; especially strangers from a foreign country who appeared on the side of the road in the middle of the night.

Her destitution that night was part of her story; her journey into the world of success and hard work to achieve her dreams.

It was dark when the truck came to a screeching halt in Manica town. They had arrived. The place was calm and deserted at the market where they were being dropped off. The smell of burnt oil and garlic stirred in the air, making Aneni salivate a little as her stomach growled in hunger. Nearby was a restaurant which made very nice food, and that's where the smell was coming from - she had learnt about it later during her stay in Manica. Aneni could not see much of the town as the street lighting was very poor.

They were dropped off and went all together to Mara's place. Gina always left her rice sacks at Mara's house as it was closer to the market, and she didn't have to carry them for a long time. Gina lived a few yards from the centre, so it made sense for her to leave the heavy stuff at Mara's. Gina said her goodbyes and wished Aneni well before walking away.

Mara's place was a two-roomed house. The house had no proper windows, but it did have a small makeshift vent which was covered by a sack. Inside, the house looked almost empty, with little to no furniture in sight.

Mara's two young children were in the other room when they arrived. A nine-year-old girl, who looked younger than her six-year-old brother, welcomed her mum.

"We have a visitor. Wake your brother up so that I can arrange the blankets," Mara told her daughter, who did just what her mother asked of her.

Aneni stood there, wondering how and where she was going to sleep as there was no bed. She always thought that her family was somewhat poor, but at that moment, her old house looked rich compared to Mara's place. Back home, they had old beds and couches and enough blankets for everyone. They were old and not so comfortable, but they were there.

She felt a deep sense of sympathy and an unexplainable pity for Mara and her children. Aneni's heart sank when she saw the two children curled up at the corner of the room with very few blankets on a seemingly uncomfortable mat. She immediately felt gratitude beyond imagination, thinking how a person in this situation had taken it upon themselves to offer her shelter, even if the shelter itself was not adequate to add another individual to it.

"Can I assist you with anything?" Aneni asked Mara. She had not left her manners back in Zimbabwe. She had carried them with her as she had been taught.

"No, thank you. I am looking for a blanket for you," Mara answered. After a few moments of Mara fumbling and rearranging things in the house, she finally told Aneni where to sleep. On the floor, Aneni slept on a sack and covered herself with a makeshift blanket made out of a Capulana, a cloth that was used by most African women to wrap themselves up when doing chores.

She carefully placed her small bag on the top of the sleeping pad and made it her pillow for the night. Mara went on to sleep with her children in the other room, and in no time, she could hear them snore away. Throughout the night, Aneni could hear drunk people fumbling outside while passing by Mara's house, and she immediately realised that Mara's house was right next to a bottle store. The way Mara and her children slept soundly amidst the noise and with the uncomfortable sleeping arrangement surprised Aneni.

"They are probably used to it," she mumbled to herself in the darkness.

Aneni struggled to catch sleep. She tossed and turned for a while. She thought back to her adventure and realised how terrifying that really was. She felt slightly accomplished by the mere fact that she had managed to cross the border into another country without a passport, accommodation or any connections. At nineteen, she had sold her teenage pleasantries for deep exploration of life and independence.

Slowly, her thoughts started to blur, and moments later, sleep managed to steal Aneni away.

Chapter 8

Thousands of people seemed to have descended in the wake of dawn. Bustling noises could be heard from everywhere, waking Aneni from her short sleep. She went outside to see people carrying baskets of produce balanced on their heads, with babies on their backs. Others pushed makeshift carts with fruits, vegetables and other goods. Some were just basking in the morning sunshine outside of dilapidated buildings. Others stood there aimlessly, putting their hands in their pockets as if they had been employed to monitor other people's movements. In no time, Aneni could see the rays of the yellow sun protruding from the mountain, a beautiful sight. In its beauty, it held untouched hopes and dreams that positively pestered Aneni's mind and soul.

Aneni had had a tough night, both physically and emotionally. She had struggled to catch sleep, and she was experiencing muscle cramps due to the hard surface that she had spent her first night in Mozambique on. Emotionally, Aneni felt sad after seeing the conditions that Mara and her children were living in. It evoked in her great empathy and compassion. At that moment, Aneni had wished to have enough material possessions to help Mara and her family as Aneni continued to be touched by Mara offering her a place to sleep. The profoundness of this gesture would stick in Aneni's mind for a long time.

As she continued to assess the new environment, Aneni paid attention to people's conversations, figuring out what language most of them spoke. After listening for a while, she concluded that most were speaking Portuguese. In fact, so many of them talked in Portuguese that Aneni wondered if it was a myth that they also spoke Sena. Aneni felt a seed of doubt growing in her mind. How was she supposed to teach people English if she didn't know their language? Was this move really the best option for her? Had she made a mistake?

Assimilation into the community would be extremely difficult due to the language barrier. Aneni briefly went back inside the house, and she heard that Mara and her children had woken up.

"Can I help with anything?" Aneni asked as Mara tried to rekindle a small fire outside to boil water for tea.

"There is nothing much to do here," Mara said, smiling at her. "You can relax. You came a long way," she added. Aneni, however, did not feel like relaxing as it meant staying alone with her doubtful thoughts. She took it upon herself to find a chore to do. She remembered her mother's wise words: *A woman is never a visitor*. It meant that a woman should always find something to do at home, even if it wasn't her home. This came from the belief that house chores will always be there: if people eat, there is a need for cooking, serving and washing dishes afterwards. So, Aneni looked around the small house, picked up a makeshift broom and started to sweep the floors. When she finished, she washed her face and went back out.

Aneni asked Mara where she could change money, and Mara directed her to the market. She wanted to change her Zimbabwean dollars into meticals. She hoped that it would be enough to sustain her for the few days, perhaps even allowing her to rent a stable place rather than staying at someone else's house.

The market itself was so quite dirty - it did not appear as if there was any maintenance of the place. Dirty water was running through small parts of the market which made it difficult for Aneni to walk without jumping to step on the dry ground. As she looked around and saw a few vendors washing their faces from a cup or a bowl, it seemed as if they had just woken up and went straight to the market without bathing. The various activities and the sellers yelling about their products in a language she didn't understand made it even more confusing for Aneni to navigate the market.

She looked around quite often, clutching her bag to her chest, wary of thieves and scammers that frequented places like this. She could understand why the thieves did what they did: life was difficult, and sometimes it was hard to make money in moral ways. However, Aneni also thought that working hard would ensure that she would never have to choose immoral practices to survive.

Aneni approached a lady who was selling homemade bread.

"Bomdia menina?" she said her greetings to Aneni.

"Makadii," Aneni responded, making sure to smile and look as respectful as possible. *Makadii* was a Shona way of saying, *How are you?* As Aneni had hoped, the lady understood her and spoke Sena back to her. She felt relief, but then her mind became blank as she was unsure how to ask for help. The lady looked at her with curious eyes and asked if Aneni wanted to buy bread, to which she said yes, but she needed to change the money into meticals first.

"Oh, cambio," the woman mumbled, and looked around and Aneni smiled as she knew that *cambio* meant *exchange*. She pointed her to a group of men. Aneni thought that they were market monitors as they appeared to be standing aimlessly with hands in their pockets. She thanked the lady and walked towards them.

For a moment, she hesitated to approach them as it was always safer to avoid groups of men, but she had no other choice. She briskly walked towards the cambio guys. As they saw her coming, they started showing wads of cash and each calling her to exchange her money with them. Most of the cambio guys spoke Shona as their trade was dominated by Zimbabwean sellers who crossed the border daily into Manica for business. With hesitation, Aneni walked to the man closest to her. She changed her money and was surprised about how little there was of it. She bought some bread from the nice lady who directed her to the man and went back to Mara's place. Although she was thankful for Mara's gesture of kindness, her top priority was to quickly rent a room and start looking for a job.

Aneni had breakfast with Mara and her kids after coming back from the market. The bread tasted delicious - it was natural, and the aroma caused nostalgia for the wheat bread that Aneni's mum made at home. The bread was accompanied by black tea, and Aneni was surprised at how full she felt after breakfast. Mara proceeded to do her business after breakfast, leaving Aneni at home alone. Mara told her that the children would come back from school. They had a routine, and they knew how to follow it through. Aneni spent the rest of the day resting and regaining her energy and planning her next move.

Early morning the following day, Aneni went out into town to check if she could find any rooms for rent. Manica was a very small town, and it did not take her long to learn how to navigate it. Most of the houses she found were more expensive than what she could possibly afford. This dampened her hopes and mood, as she began to feel the need to move from Mara's place, not only because of the discomfort but because she felt she was a burden to an already burdened person. She realised that to move out, she needed a job.

During that time, the economic crisis that the Zimbabwean nation was facing caused a lot of destitution from the nationals in other countries. This meant that people in the neighbouring countries were not very accepting of Zimbabwean people. Suddenly, the once breadbasket of Africa was pitied by everyone around them. The stereotypes were mounting, putting even more pressure on the Zimbabweans who sought to make an honest living and sustain their families. The stereotypes and generality of people made it difficult for foreigners to navigate and assimilate within other countries.

The only weapon Aneni possessed was her excellent command of the English language. She had resorted to using a very polished accent to captivate and attract attention that could hide the fact that she was a Zimbabwean. She felt that she possessed a peculiar power that would enable acceptance and cause people to look at her differently. Each time she approached affluent people, she made sure to use her British accent. It was so polished that most people would stare and listen to her voice, even though some did not even comprehend much of what she said. She acted well, presenting a black exterior with a white interior. In most cases, it served its purpose as parents described how proud they would be if their children could be as eloquent as Aneni.

After doing the rounds, looking for an affordable room to rent, she eventually returned to Mara's place, with no good news. She told Mara of her day. Mara said she

would stay another night but could not accommodate her
further than that. The hospitality between them had
suddenly changed from warm to somehow tense. Aneni
could not comprehend what could have possibly upset
Mara, but at least she could sleep for the night. Thoughts
lingered in her mind, and she felt sad that Mara was not
happy for a reason unknown to her. She wondered if she
had done something wrong, but she couldn't think of what
that could be. She had been well behaved and had offered
to do chores and help in the house several times. *What was
it?* She wondered. *What made Mara unhappy with me?*

Later in the day, Aneni went to the pit toilet. It was
a kind of toilet that made one see everything in the pit. As
she entered, she inevitably looked in it. Then something
made her heart skip a bit; something that made her sick in
the stomach. At the bottom of the pit, she saw a tiny body.
A baby, her mind told her. She looked away and quickly
dismissed the thought. *It's probably a doll*, she told herself,
but she didn't really believe it.

Even though Aneni brushed off the incident, her
heart sank whenever she thought about it. At nineteen years
of age, she had heard stories of girls having unplanned
pregnancies, only to end up aborting or dumping the babies.
With the values that she always had, she considered this to
be a heinous crime that God might not forgive. However,
she couldn't help but feel empathy for the girls, who made
a mistake or might've been forced to sleep with men against
their will. In most cases, the girls dumping and aborting
their babies was a response to the denial of help from the
baby's father. Other times, it was because the act would have
happened with someone married or way older than them,
and the prospects of having a future with them would be

bleak. Still, no matter how empathetic she was towards the troubled girls, she couldn't get the image of the baby out of her mind. *Maybe it was a miscarriage*, she thought to herself. The sight was haunting, and as much as Aneni wished to dismiss it, it kept reappearing in her mind. After that incident, she feared using the toilet and to even look in its direction. She decided not to ask Mara about it.

She spent the rest of the day thinking about the standards that society put on women. Society was complex, intensely complex, and it did not allow people to be.

Society had its standards and expectations, and if someone wanted to be respected, they had to uphold these standards. If they didn't, they would be rejected, ostracised, stereotyped, neglected and subjected to severe scrutiny.

In those days, the traditional expectation for a young girl would start at finishing school and getting a job. A job that would not intimidate the man; a simple job, a job that would help the family but not let the woman be independent in her own means. Young girls were expected to have nurturing professions such as becoming teachers, nurses and secretaries. They were told that they were good enough to put something on the table and help their spouse, but not good enough to run businesses, become engineers, build big affluent homes and buy themselves expensive cars.

Following completion of simple education and getting a simple job, girls were then expected to get married and settle down as quickly as possible. Within months of getting married, the girl should become pregnant and have a child, two years later another child, and then another, and then another. The girl should hope for her children to be men, so they could have big jobs and big dreams that the girl herself was not expected to have.

After wandering around the neighbourhood, deep in her thoughts, Aneni returned to Mara's house. She felt discomfort as she entered the place - when one was no longer welcome, it was difficult to relax. She sat down on the floor and, as usual, asked if she could help with anything, and Mara told her that there was nothing to do. Then suddenly, Mara turned around and looked her right in the eyes.

"Were you pregnant? Is that why you are running away from Zimbabwe?" she asked.

"No!" Aneni answered, shocked, and needed a second to collect herself. "No man has yet touched me, and I certainly did not run away from Zimbabwe! Why would you think that of me?" she asked, angry that Mara would think something like that about her. Mara, however, also looked angry.

"Maybe because there is a foetus in the toilet pit!" she answered in an angry whisper as if even saying that out loud could get her in trouble. She clearly assumed that it was Aneni who had aborted and dumped the baby in the toilet. Another sombre moment for Aneni, as she then could not lie to herself anymore and confirmed that it was not a doll but actually a baby. Well, this explained why Mara wanted her gone.

Mara let out a sigh in disbelief that Aneni was still a virgin. Aneni's heart continued to sink, and she shook her head. She did not wish to battle in her defence any further, realising that it was her word against Mara's. She sighed.

"If you want me to go to the doctor to check if I'm lying, then I am happy to go with you," she said. Mara did not wish to pursue this further, but the feeling of distrust followed them that day. Before Aneni went to sleep, Mara came to her.

"There is a young lady, three houses down," Mara said. "She put on some weight, and she was ill today. She was taken to the doctor, and some people heard her talk about 'her baby' and how sorry she was. Poor girl," Mara finished speaking and looked at Aneni, who nodded in response. "You can stay as long as you need," Mara then added before turning around and going to her room. Aneni took a deep breath, relief washing over her. All was well... at least for now.

Chapter 9

"How much can you afford?" asked Senhora Fernanda Antonio.

"I do not have much. I can afford 200 meticals," responded Aneni.

"There is one vacant room at the back of my property, but it needs a thorough cleaning," said Senhora Fernanda. "The room was last used two years ago by my husband's brother. Since then, no one has bothered to go in there, let alone clean it."

Senhora Fernanda was a stout, bold lady who commanded respect. She did not appear to smile a lot. Aneni didn't care about Senhora Fernanda's looks as long as she could secure the accommodation. The outlook of the house wasn't the worst. It was clear that it was built with very strong material, and it appeared to resemble old architecture, one which could easily pass as a monument, a historical icon in the next few years to come. The entrance was an arched veranda with a stoop where Senhora Fernanda's children sat while looking at their mum. Aneni had been looking for a place for almost two weeks, and this was the first time she could afford it. She agreed on the rent price and asked when she could move in.

"Whenever you want," was the answer.

Aneni went back to Mara's and collected her belongings. She thanked Mara for the gesture of love that she had shown by letting her stay. Aneni pressed a 20 Metical note in Mara's hand and showed her a smile, a smile of gratitude. Mara thanked her and wished her the best in her journey.

The first thing she did was clean the room. The shackles of dust were dancing in the air, making her cough constantly. At that moment, her choices were limited and what mattered was having a roof over her head. The room was big, but there was nothing in it, except an old wardrobe with a cracked mirror and a slightly broken door. The lace curtain on the window had seen better days; and when she attempted to draw it, speckles of dust flew in the air, landing on her face. She did not worry much about the curtain. She removed it and thought that she would wash it later. The window was on the west side, and when the sun was setting, the rays would penetrate through the glass lighting up her room. At night when the moon was bright, she would stand there looking at the beauty it exuded. The magnificence of nature brought a mood of calmness onto Aneni even when her life was tough.

With little money she had left, Aneni went to Kaunjika, an informal clothing market which sold second-hand stuff from abroad. She picked one sky blue duvet cover and a simple old blanket. She could not afford a stove, neither was she used to the coal style stove named *fogao*, which was a very common cooking aid in Mozambique. For the days to come, Aneni will have to live on bread and juice.

Aneni moved into Senhora Fernanda's room on a Friday. The weekend was long, and she sat on the blankets in her room, putting together a few lesson plans for students that she was yet to find. Aneni held so much faith in her dream that no matter how rough the road seemed, she did not stop believing and planned as if all was smooth. A rare and peculiar kind of trait especially coming from a young and beautiful woman.

Aneni did not want to waste any time. On Saturday afternoon, she set out to the community. She went around the neighbourhood knocking at doors, announcing that she was an English teacher and was looking for people interested in learning the language. Aneni never forgot to speak perfect polished English as a tool to market herself. She also factored in the importance of looking well-groomed and dressing modestly. She felt that people associated being well-spoken as also being groomed and decent. She knew that her appearance would be the first thing people noticed about her and it could determine whether they wished to hear what she had to say or not.

Most of the people she approached were mesmerised by her fluent English. Parents wished their children could speak English at such a level. In some homes, she would get a warm welcome, followed by diplomatic dismissal.

I will talk to my husband and let you know, meant they don't have the guts to tell you no themselves.

My children learn English at school, meant they don't want *you* teaching them.

I will think about it, meant they already made up their mind.

In other homes, she would face abrupt one-sentence responses like *not interested* or *no thanks.* Those kinds of responses annoyed her the most as she could not figure out what she did wrong. Each rejection was a learning experience for Aneni as she reflected on how she could've acted. Aneni felt that through the experience, she was learning valuable life lessons about not getting everything easily.

A couple of people said to come again next week and that kept Aneni hopeful. On a few occasions, she would knock, and very handsome young men would open the door, and she would immediately feel shy. Aneni was also aware that some men would potentially want to take advantage of her under the pretences of being interested in her lessons. She told herself that she would not teach a man who lived alone to avoid possible dangers. At the time, finding a boyfriend was not in Aneni's plans or vocabulary. She meant business and she focused on business only.

Aneni did not give up, and on the following Monday, she went to a different suburb called Piscina. Piscina was more affluent. It was a suburb where bank managers and businesspeople lived. The houses were posh with some needing her to ring the intercom to announce her presence. The downside of the intercom was that the owners would ask what she wanted without having to open the gate. This compromised her marketing strategy as she would not be able to show her physical confidence in her pitch. The journey continued and while Aneni looked for students; she left no stone unturned.

By the end of that week Aneni had managed to secure three families interested in their children learning the English language. Elated by that, she went on to prepare materials for the first lesson. She did not have much, except a few English books that she had sneaked in her bag and about two of them were elementary English books. She also had put down a good plan and a makeshift syllabus that would help her students catch up with the language. She even went to the local secondary school called Jecua to ask for some stationery, which she got from the head teacher, Mr Cardoso. The head teacher appeared amazed to see a young and beautiful girl working so hard to earn a living. Mr Cardoso also expressed his interest in having his children learn the English language. Mr Cardoso gave her his business card and asked if she could call the following day after he had spoken to his wife.

The following Monday she was up and ready to go and teach her one-hour sessions to the three families.

By devising her teaching plan and strategy, she succeeded in engaging her students. She did not charge a lot because she did not want to scare people off- she needed money. Her teaching strategy was mainly pictorial. She used images to explain things in English because there was a language barrier from her side as most affluent families only spoke Portuguese. Most professionals had hailed from other provinces which did not speak Sena. Not only did this help her students understand but in the process, she also learnt bits and pieces of Portuguese.

Soon she found joy in teaching the children English. It was a delight to her and besides the money there was a deeper fulfilment that engulfed her whole being. She was also able to secure a few adult students who were more difficult and intimidating to teach. She even went to teach the regional commander at his home. She would always tremble while speaking to him as she felt small next to him. Regardless, she soldiered on and her confidence grew. She continued to sprout like a flower in the mornings of spring after the dew had fallen.

Chapter 10

The few weeks that followed were quite eventful. Word had gone out in the town that a young, beautiful girl was teaching English in the area. Many people started to develop an interest in learning English and more referrals came for Aneni. Of note was her charisma and charm that most of the families she taught fell in love with. Aneni had a very soft aura, and her voice was gentle yet strong enough to make a bold statement. She always put her head on the side when she spoke to children and adults. For many, that was a sign of pure humbleness, the capability to reduce herself before others. She learnt a lot from the families as well- including her growing understanding of Portuguese. One of the families were Indian, and they would give her Indian food at weekends. Some families would invite her to family events, dinners, birthdays, and even weddings. Many parents felt that she represented a strong, disciplined and intelligent young woman who if afforded an opportunity would rise high in life. Her character was admirable, her principles and values enviable.

However, when a flower blooms so are the many insects that scramble to suck nectar from it. A lot of men, both young and old, thought that Aneni would be a good prey for their perverted desires and tried to lure her into having a relationship with them. Although there were also a few who probably would have wanted her for the right reasons. Aneni's mind was fixated on her dream. She got rid of any thoughts of getting into a relationship. Entertaining men while she lived alone was not going to facilitate her dream in any way. Not only that, but she also wanted to maintain her principle of not indulging in intimacy with any man until she got married. She felt that she would fall into the hands of a man who would not share the same vision as her and perhaps derail her dream.

Days went by and life remained monotonous. Aneni had a usual routine - she would wake up, bathe, eat, and go out to teach. At this time the work was overwhelming as many people had approached her to teach their families. She was constantly fatigued. Something that she had not envisioned when she was booking all these lessons. For her; a new booking meant more money and coming closer to her dream.

She realised she needed a better plan to manage the times and the walking that was involved in her going from one house to another. The money was rolling in, but not enough to save for her dream, or at least not as quickly as she wanted it to. At the end of the month, the money was just enough for her rent, food and a few things but not enough remaining in savings. Although her work was giving her enough to live on, it did not make sense for her to continue without a better plan. She then started to look for a more professional English teaching post. It had proven to be a difficult job as Manica was a small town, and there weren't many opportunities in it. She also only had her Ordinary Level certificate and nothing else to make her a candidate for a better position.

One day, when Aneni had just finished her last session of the day and as usual she walked home alone. She was used to walking home alone even at night. She felt safe as the area was small and not synonymous with crime. It appeared harmless. On this day while walking home she saw a car parked on the side of the road. The car looked new and it had tinted windows. Aneni had seen that car doing the rounds around the town, but she had never thought much about it. She did not contemplate much about who was in the car and what that car was doing parked at the side of the road at night. As she walked past it, she heard a window being wound down.

"Teacher, how are you?" a hoarse voice asked. Aneni hesitated for a moment while she tried to figure out who the person was. She could not recognise the face or the voice. However, she relaxed a little bit because, clearly, the person knew who she was. "I am fine, how are you?" she responded rather coyly.

"We're fine!" Aneni realised that there was another man in the car. Both of them looked like they were in their late fifties.

"We can offer you a ride to where you are going", the first man said. "It's too late for a beautiful woman like yourself to walk by herself," he added. He wore a scotch shirt and appeared harmless. She was hesitant, but then she noticed that the other man was the father of one of her students. She relaxed immediately and accepted their offer, entering the car.

The ride to her home was not long as it probably took just ten minutes to reach there by car and about thirty-five minutes walking. During the short ride, the two men asked Aneni about Zimbabwe, stating how devastating the change of circumstances in the country had. They mentioned how many Mozambicans survived in Zimbabwe during their own political unrest, famine and drought. They recognised how Zimbabwe was once the breadbasket of Africa where people in the neighbouring countries sought refuge in times of trouble and unrest. Aneni agreed with the fact that the situation was dire. She believed that one day it would get better and Zimbabwe would see better days again.

The two men dropped Aneni at her place. She thanked them for the ride and tiptoed to her room. As she was fumbling in her handbag to get keys for her door, she heard Senhora Fernanda calling her from the veranda. Senhora Fernanda had a habit of leaving her lounge curtain open so she could see events happening outside. It seemed Senhora Fernanda noticed the car that had dropped her off.

"Please do not get into those men's cars," she said hurriedly in broken Shona. "They are being accused of murder of an eight-year-old boy." She shook her head. "And they did it. I know they did. They do kill children and take their heads and other organs to South Africa for money. That's where they got that car which you came in," Senhora Fernanda grabbed Aneni's arms and shook her a little. "Do not eat anything at their house when you go and teach his children. Do not take lifts with them. People here have closets full of skeletons," she said and let Aneni go. Perplexed and scared, Aneni felt as if her life had come to a standstill. The thought of her being killed and sold to South Africa meant that her family would never be able to trace her. She needed time to absorb the news as she cried bitterly inside and fear immediately crept into her mind.

"Thank you for letting me know. They saw me walking and offered to drop me home, and I thought there was no problem, I thought I didn't have to be scared," Aneni said in a trembling voice.

"Don't trust these people, please. What will your family say if you just disappear?" Aneni nodded. She felt as if she was in a daze when she grabbed her bag and left for her room. The fear whispered inside her, a little voice reminding her how close she was to becoming a victim.

The days after the incident were sombre. Aneni developed paranoia. She doubted anything and everything. She became more careful as she feared for her life and she did not want to die before achieving her goals.

In the face of fear, Aneni turned to her religion. She had managed to find a respectable church Forward in Faith. Most of the people there spoke Sena. The church became a good distraction from the worldly woes for Aneni - the people were warm and would invite her to their homes for lunch or dinner. She began feeling a sense of community and belonging.

The services were quite long as they included singing, testimonies, preaching and then more singing and dancing. She particularly enjoyed the singing and dancing part. All sermons were conducted in Portuguese with a Sena translator, which made Aneni feel included.

The lunches she was invited to were enjoyable, especially at Pastor De Souza's family. There was a housemaid named Sara. Sara was a great cook as she made food with all her heart. Aneni particularly enjoyed the yellow rice accompanied by a chicken stew - it tasted divine. She enjoyed the lunches even more as she was unable to cook hot meals at her own place. Even after Aneni could afford to buy a small stove, she did not feel the need to do it. She didn't feel like she lived at her place as she was rarely there except for sleeping. She also considered this part of her life as a passing stage, and she did not want to waste any money on it.

The people at Pastor De Souza's home were very warm. They enjoyed listening to her speak English and that pressed the pomp in Aneni, humble kind of pomp or rather good pride. Sara would admiringly look at Aneni when she talked, Aneni would blush from within as the small moments of fame engulfed her.

Although Aneni had a lot on her mind, her life in Manica seemed a little bleak as it was composed only of working and trying to save money. Life started to make little sense, as the prospects of getting a breakthrough job in the town were close to none. Living from hand to mouth was not what she looked forward to as she wanted to save money to pursue her dream. She had many students, but she charged very little for a lot of work she did which caused her to have little to no savings.

When she was in Manica, she had also effortlessly made friends with American and British expatriates, most of whom were official English teachers to the local high school. The expatriates were contracted by the Voluntary Service Overseas organisation (VSO). She became friendly with Marta who came from California. Marta was a twenty-seven-year-old white lady. She was very tall and quite warm and humble. She liked going out to the Discoteca on Fridays, which was parallel to Aneni's customs and principles.

Marta would scarcely succeed in convincing her to tag along with her to the Discoteca. She would even pay for her entrada fee and refreshments. However, for Aneni, the whole experience was a drag. On one occasion, Aneni found herself sleeping in the Discoteca to the slight dismay of her new friend. Later, Marta found it funny that Aneni had managed to fall asleep in such a noisy place.

It became an inside joke, and they would laugh about it often. Going to the Discoteca was, however, good for Aneni. It managed to divert her attention from misery and thoughts of fear of the unknown future.

At times Marta would be invited to official government dinner parties which Aneni was her tag along. In Mozambique, people were quite liberal and they did not have much reservation in expressing themselves which was a long way of saying that they loved dancing. The most popular dance in Mozambique was called *Passada*. The *Passada* was a sensual dance that could only be danced by two people, a man and a woman. The man took charge of directing the dance while putting one arm on the lady's shoulder. The other hand would hold her hand, extended outward. The waist and the movement of the feet commanded the dance. The sensual connotations come from the spectator who might not be privy to the custom. The dance was considered perfectly normal, and the Mozambicans did not think of it as sensual in any way.

Men would ask Aneni to dance but she often refused as this was out of her comfort zone.

"Relax, it's not a big deal," Marta would tell her.

"To me, it is," Aneni would answer, not giving any explanation. Certain boundaries in life could not be crossed, and she always felt comfortable about her choices.

They would disagree on a lot of little things and soon the dynamism that Marta had brought to her life began to die out. She went back to her drawing board to re-strategise.

She needed more money, and she could not get it in Manica. She needed a boat that could take her to the UK, where her dreams would be within reach. She needed to focus and work hard. These forced disco expeditions were certainly not part of the equation. After hours of contemplating, she finally made a decision.

She was leaving Manica.

Chapter 11

Aneni arrived in Beira on a very hot Sunday afternoon. Her trip from Manica had been uneventful. Some parts of the road were quite bumpy and dusty. On her arrival, she looked powdered on her face and her clothes had a lot of dust. A two-seater on the bus was accommodating four people, and she travelled squashed like sardines. The heat was unbearable. When she opened the bus windows, the dust gushed inside. In her mind, she wondered why the road, known as the *Beira Corridor*, was so unkempt.

Beira was the second capital city of Mozambique. The route was the main road and railway linking the neighbouring countries, Zimbabwe, Zambia, and Malawi, to the port of Beira on the Indian Ocean. She had read and learnt about the Beira Corridor in school and expected it to be more pleasant.

At checkpoints, the conductor would corruptly give the officers money so that they wouldn't complain about the capacity of the bus. All that did not matter to her, at least she was starting a new adventure, with the hope that this time around she would succeed in getting a good job that paid in United States Dollars. So broad was the will, so narrow the means.

Beira was the hub for business activities, industry and tourism. Life was also more expensive and accelerated than the one in Manica. Most Zimbabwean informal traders came to Beira to buy second-hand clothes in bales for resell in Zimbabwe. This business contributed significantly to the upkeep of many households.

As she stepped out of the bus, she was greeted by many vendors who sold anything she could think of. She witnessed clothes being displayed on the floor at almost every corner of the town. Shoes, shirts, handbags and more were neatly laid on the ground for people to buy. On the side, other people would sell food, including vegetables, fruits, and small packs of salt, rice or sugar.

In Zimbabwe, clothing markets and fruit and vegetable markets stood in designated areas with properly allocated space, so this was a new experience for Aneni. Clothes were mainly sold at flea markets, where people would hire their stand to sell from, whereas fruits and vegetables were sold at what was known as *green markets*. Shocked at seeing this kind of market, she wondered what else would be different in this new city.

Portuguese was the main language used by almost everyone in Beira. It was no longer a big hurdle for Aneni because she had mastered basic Portuguese during her time in Manica. She was sure that she would be able to navigate Beira with the broken Portuguese and some English.

The idea of moving to Beira came after Aneni wondered how she could perhaps earn more with her English teaching. She had spoken to a few people that she met on her outings with Marta and most of them felt that she stood a better chance in a bigger city. Beira came highly recommended. Her options for any other job were quite limited and exploring Beira could mean more money and more people needing English lessons. She was wary of the high cost of living there, but she felt she had to try.

She had also met a friend in Manica who had promised that she would accommodate her for a short time until she found a new place and a job. Her name was Mazza.

Mazza was a young lady whom Aneni had met one afternoon in Manica while having lunch at a restaurant.

Many people were drawn to Aneni because she spoke English. She was even friends with white people known in Sena as *Vazungu* or *Branco* in Portuguese. Mazza joined Aneni for lunch, and they shared contacts. Or more accurately Mazza gave Aneni her phone number and told her to call if she was ever in Beira. Aneni at that time did not have a phone. This gave her good hope that for a change, she could go to a new place where someone was waiting for her. She did not have to become destitute or wander in a big city. She decided to move shortly after.

Downtown was a Telecomunicacoes de Mozambique (TDM) store, which she used to call Mazza. The system used prepaid cards to make calls, or one could pay at the counter for the minutes they wanted to speak for. Aneni paid for one minute to make the call - money was scarce and splashing was not an option.

She dialled Mazza's number, and it rang three times before she picked. Aneni could hear Mazza on the other side and eagerly announced that she had arrived in Beira and was downtown. Mazza responded and she said that she would come to fetch her within the next hour. They arranged to meet just outside the TDM building. Aneni stood outside with her bags that she had brought from Zimbabwe.

The tiredness had descended upon her physically and mentally. Physically, because of the long journey. Mentally, because in her mind she was hatching a plan of action. Aneni could wait an hour. She desired nothing more but to go home, take a shower, eat and sleep. So, Aneni waited.

One hour passed and turned to three hours but there was no sign of Mazza. At one point, Aneni had smiled at a lady who was passing as she thought it was her. She went back inside TDM to make another call, but this time the number was unfortunately not reachable. The pain of hearing the *ting ting ting* sound was too much for Aneni. She waited one more hour until it dawned on her that Mazza was not coming.

Outside it was getting dark and the security guard at the TDM asked if she was okay. The adrenaline of anxiety, fear and tiredness ensued on Aneni. She was uneasy and confused. She had heard Beira was very dangerous and full of thieves. A lot of women were raped, and their goods were stolen in broad daylight. Suddenly she realised that she was standing in the dark on her own, in the city where she knew no one. She was helpless once again.

The security guard had noticed the fear and tears welling down Aneni's cheeks.

"O Que se passa moca?" he asked, meaning *what's the matter, young girl?* With much difficulty, Aneni struggled to explain that she had no place to go. Amazingly, the security guard understood but he had thought it was a boyfriend who had stood her up. *Whatever makes society think that the tears of a woman have to be associated with a man*, Aneni thought. "Espera aqui", the security guard said, which meant *wait here* so she waited. She wanted to laugh the laughter of weariness because she thought where would she even go? She couldn't even tell east from west in this city. Everything was hollow and carried no direction.

The security guard went inside and spoke to the lady who attended the desk for the evening shift. The security guard beckoned Aneni inside the TDM. The lady came out of her cubicle and greeted her with an empathetic look. It was not the look of someone receiving a customer.

"Hi, I'm Marlene," the woman said. Her English was perfect, and Aneni felt relief. "I am sorry that your friend stood you up. It happens a lot here. People are not genuine nowadays," Marlene added.

"I thought she really meant she would accommodate me, otherwise I would not be in this position," Aneni struggled to explain.

"That's okay. I can accommodate you for the night, but you need to see what you can do tomorrow. I do not have a big place, and I live with my maid and my child," she explained. Marlene was finishing her shift at eight, which meant Aneni had to wait for at least an hour but that did not matter for Aneni as she had somewhere to lay for the night. Marlene became her saviour for the night and she was not be sceptical of her either as she seemed kind.

Marlene helped Aneni carry her bags to her car, a white Volkswagen Golf. Darkness had descended upon them but the streetlights lit the city of Beira as if it was day. As they drove to Marlene's house in Pontagea, Aneni felt a temporary sense of relief and security. Pontagea appeared to be a more affluent area. Seemingly an area for the middle class, the bourgeoisie because of the bigger houses and leafiness. She wondered whether Marlene's salary was enough to live in an area like that, but then she reminded herself that it was not her business to probe or even to speculate.

When they got to her house, Aneni realised that Marlene lived on the annexe at the back of the main house. The annexe had two bedrooms and a small lounge with a kitchen. She lived with her eight-year-old son and a nanny who was taking care of him. The son was already sleeping when they arrived but the nanny was still awake. She greeted Aneni with cheer and warmth while taking her bags to the other room. She then warmed coconut rice, fish and lettuce salad for Aneni and Marlene. Aneni took the time to have a quick shower before she ate. The food was warm and delicious, a rare treat especially after six months of having bread and juice. She only on a few occasions could afford some chips and chicken at the local restaurants in Manica and the occasional visits to the pastor De Souza's house and gatherings.

"You know Zimbabweans are marginalised in this country. People feel that you are only here to sell pillows and duvets, ruining the streets," Marlene said. "And some beautiful women like you are apparently known to be pursuing prostitution," she added.

"Oh, that's so sad," she responded, shocked by Marlene's words. "Zimbabweans are very educated and hardworking. Of course, our economy is not favourable at this moment. People do try to do anything to better themselves," she said. Emotions were starting to build inside Aneni. She never heard anyone being so mean about her people to her face.

"Oh, I understand that, but you can't change what people think about others," Marlene responded, bringing the fork of rice to her mouth. "What are you planning to do to sustain yourself in Beira?"

Aneni explained her plan to Marlene, talking about her hardships and her hard work to achieve her dream, but Marlene interrupted her.

"I think it will be better if you say you are South African rather than Zimbabwean," she said suddenly. "That way people will respect you more and warm up to you much easier you know." She must've seen disgust on Aneni's face as she added, "Try, and you will see."

Marlene allowed her to stay two more days at her house. During the day, she would go out to look for a room to rent. The first day was futile as no accommodation fitted her meagre budget. Most people told her that she could only find accommodation within her range in a very dilapidated area of Beira called Mataquane. She even went on to check some rooms there. The houses were made of mud, and the flooring was almost permanently dusty. There were no toilets as people in the area used the bush. For bathing, there were makeshift thatched enclosures that stunk. Aneni was told some people urinated in there.

Immediately, it dawned on Aneni that she would not be able to stay in dilapidated houses or better rooms in better areas. She was not necessarily looking for affluence, but rather cleanliness, electricity and good sanitation. Although her budget could not accommodate better, she still felt that she had a basic standard to uphold.

Weary, tired and afraid, she could not fathom how this situation would pan out. The following day, she was expected to move out of Marlene's house. She did not wish to be a menace to someone who had welcomed and accommodated her at a very dire moment. It would be ungrateful of her.

That night, as she pondered her next move, Marlene asked if she had made a plan so she could move.

"No, I haven't. The houses are expensive, and I cannot afford any of the rooms," Aneni said. To her surprise, Marlene smiled.

"I thought that might've been the case. I spoke to someone who is letting out a security guard quarters. The owners of the house are in Portugal and the guard does not need the room because he goes to his home when he finishes work," she explained.

"Oh, that's great! Thank you so much for helping me," Aneni said. A glimmer of hope and relief afforded Aneni a smile, a smile that had become so expensive leading to that moment.

Chapter 12

Rock of Ages cleft for me,
Let me hide myself in thee
Let the water, and the blood,
From thy wounded side which flowed
Be of sin the double cure,
Save from wrath and make me pure

Not the labours of my hands
Can fulfil thy law's demands
Could the zeal no respite know
Could my tear forever flow
All for sin could not atone
Thou must save, and thou alone

Nothing in my hand I bring,
Simply to the cross I cling
Naked come to thee for dress
Helpless, look to thee for grace
Foul, I to the fountain fly
Wash me Saviour or I die
Rock of Ages, cleft for me
Let me hide myself in thee

(United Methodist Hymnal, 1989)

Aneni sang *Rock of Ages* in her heart as she unpacked her few possessions in the security guard quarters. The song brought immense nostalgia and memories of her family back home in Zimbabwe. Soon, tears welled down her smooth cheeks. She recognised that she needed a supreme being to hail her forward as she sometimes lacked the power, the wisdom, and conducive conditions to run her life.

There was not much for her to unpack. The room was compact and did not have any form of furniture. In it, she put her old blue duvet which she had bought in Manica. It had surely seen better days, but at that time it was serving its purpose. She also brought a cream blanket. She carefully folded the blanket into two to form a mattress and she covered herself with the duvet. It was during summer in Beira, and it was extremely hot, so she did not require a lot of blankets. Outside was a single toilet with an overhead shower in the same room. It was all concrete inside the bathroom. It was still better than the place in Mataquane and she made an effort to clean it and ensure it was always clean. She did not have a stove so she resorted to the same Manica arrangement where she would only live on juice and bread.

Days and months went by. Aneni had secured some students in Beira with her new identity as a South African. She tried to dissociate herself from being called Zimbabwean and as Marlene predicted, there was a warmer response from people. The Mozambicans regard South Africa as the Europe of Africa, all glory was bestowed upon it. Therefore, the mention of being South African made most people very warm in the hope that one day she would facilitate for them to visit. What they thought about her did not matter at that moment because her focus remained and she wanted to reach her goal whatever it took. In this case, it was taking her to denounce the very identity that she had so much pride in, masquerading under a false name. As painful as it was, it needed to be done.

She continued to teach, and her fluency in Portuguese grew even stronger. It was still a little broken but she would get around and communicate. She made friends with a young married woman, a student at the local university. Her name was Fidelina.

Fidelina was married to a man called Lito. Lito was fourteen years older than her Fidelina and very wealthy. She had confided in her several times that Lito was seeing other girls, and that she was contemplating divorce. Aneni did not have any wise words to offer her friend as she was not married. She could only offer a shoulder to cry on. Fidelina made Aneni's life in Beira more interesting. On weekends she would take her out with her family to eat at restaurants and spend some time watching TV at her house. Fidelina was very fluent in English, and she enjoyed hanging around with Aneni to show off her English prowess. She would proudly introduce her to her friends and colleagues.

"My South African friend," she would say. This made Aneni feel guilty about her lies, but she persisted. Fidelina became her family during the time she stayed in Beira.

The place that Aneni lived was just a few minutes away from the beach. Many weekends she would go and take long walks on the beach, watching fishermen at work, casting their nets to catch fish which they would sell to the fish vendors. She particularly enjoyed the sunsets and the reflection of the sun in the sea. It brought a feeling of peace and tranquillity into her heart.

Life in Beira was quite dynamic. She knew that her greatest agenda was not being met. The money she earned from teaching people in their homes was not bringing forth the desired sheaves. In the blink of an eye, one year had already passed and yet she still lived from hand to mouth with almost no savings. Her life was not promising to be better despite the much-anticipated business flow of her English lessons in a bigger city.

One day she had a dream. In that dream, Aneni was crossing a river where the water was very clear. As she was crossing the river, a snake appeared from nowhere and she woke up. The dream troubled Aneni the whole day. She was not sure what it meant. As vivid as it was, she felt that the dream was not just a dream but a revelation of some sort. "Mum used to say clear water is a good dream, but this sudden appearance of snake worries me", she thought. Dreams made a big spiritual impact on her, growing up there were always connotations and revelations of the future which came by through dreams. She did not take dreams very lightly. "I will let this dream lie, whatever its meaning, who cares after all", she muttered to herself.

The following day, she went to give English lessons to one of her students. When she arrived, the student that she was teaching was very busy so she could not attend lessons on that day. As Aneni walked back towards the gate, she saw United States Dollar notes on the ground. As thoughts were rushing through her mind, she quickly picked up the notes. Her heart was beating and wondered whether she should ask if someone had dropped it or if she should just take it. She chose the latter, pocketing the money which added up to two hundred dollars.

For Aneni, the two hundred dollars would give her a good start in life as it converted to almost five thousand

Meticals at the time. This much money would do a lot of good to her financial stability - she could pay ten months of rent with it. Her heart was beating at the new windfall that had seemingly come from the heavens as she had never picked such an amount of money in her lifetime. It made sense to her that the dream she had had the night before was a premonition of this. However, she wondered whether the part of her dream with a snake meant anything at all - crystal-clear water was a good sign, but the snake was not. She walked to the house where she was to give her next lesson.

Her lesson with the other student did not go well, as she was distracted, thinking and pondering about how she would spend the money effectively. She brushed through the lesson by giving the student a brief recap of the previous lesson, did a few conjunctions, and then tasked the student to read a story that she had prepared. The student was then supposed to then write a summary of comprehension from it.

"Are you okay, Professora?" asked the student. Professora means a female teacher in Portuguese.

The student had noticed that the teacher was not her usual self. She would normally take her time while teaching, ensuring that the student comprehends everything that she had planned. She also encouraged more practice sessions, where the student would have a dialogue with the teacher.

"I am well. I just have a slight headache, but I will be fine," she answered.

"Oh, Professora, you can go home if you are not feeling well," the student said, mixing some Portuguese and

English in his sentence. Aneni obliged and promised that she would catch up better on the next lesson.

As she was walking back to her place, Aneni saw the couple from the house she picked two hundred dollars from driving around. They had just gone round the roundabout when they noticed her and pulled over. Immediately, her heart sank and as she witnessed this, she was plotting the most honest answer she would give if the money she picked belonged to them. She could not change the route, neither could she run away. She gathered courage and put a smile on her face. She did not have a small handbag, so she had carefully stored the money in the safety of her tiny bra.

The lady smiled back and greeted Aneni, asking if she wanted a lift home. Aneni jumped in the car, thankful that she would not have to walk back. They drove to their house and asked if she could come in for a minute. Already, at the time, Aneni's mind was reeling, a mix of feelings, pain, embarrassment, weariness and disappointment. She already knew that the cat had come out of the bag.

Just like any kind of situation, one should always leave room for the benefit of the doubt. She sat in the lounge, and the woman quickly announced that they were missing some money, two hundred dollars. It was Aneni and one of the housekeepers whom they suspected, so they were both in the questioning dock.

Aneni could not surrender easily - she was adamant that she did not see that kind of money. Each time, her thoughts were focused on the things she would do with that kind of money rather than the integrity she would maintain by admitting to picking the notes. The questioning became futile for the couple so they resorted to taking both Aneni and the male housekeeper Mainato to the local police station for further questioning and investigation.

The police did not take long. Two female police officers took Aneni into a private room and two male police took Mainato.

They searched Aneni's trousers and checked her shirt, and they found nothing. They asked her to take off her clothes and shivers, trembling and sweating ensued. Right then, the police realised she had the money. It was obvious from her body language. A sense of deep sadness and pain sunk inside her heart. She did not know what to say or what to do so she kept quiet. She feared sleeping in the cells. Tears welled down her smooth cheeks, remembering where she had come from and why this had happened. The couple decided not to press charges, so she was free to go but that meant no more working with them.

"Mas ela e Bonita," she heard one of the policewoman say as she was leaving the police station. *But she is beautiful.* Perhaps they were wondering why a beautiful girl like her would ever find herself in such a situation. Aneni found herself wondering the same thing.

It became clear to Aneni that the dream had come to pass.

The future suddenly became bleak as it dawned on Aneni that Beira did not seem to be reaping the desired results. For the next two months, Aneni contemplated her next move. Life became unbearable and painful. She never looked forward to the next day because the next day did not seem to be promising greener pastures.

She took comfort in immersing herself in reading the St Gideon's pocket bible which she had carried with her from home. She read the bible from the first page to the last page. Some parts of it were interesting, encouraging and promising. Aneni was taken and deeply strengthened by the story of the Israelites, the journey they partook from Egypt to Canaan. This story had carried her from Zimbabwe into Mozambique. She felt her life depicted on a grand level: the drive to seek greener pastures, but instead facing a block of unending trouble and suffering, to the point where one could easily have given up altogether. Aneni held on to her dream and refused to give up, akin to the fact that she would eventually find a breakthrough. In that breakthrough, she would continue to work hard to honestly earn enough to forge ahead. However, right now she wasn't sure if that would be enough. She wasn't sure if she was enough.

Chapter 13

A very chilly morning greeted Beira on the exact day that Aneni was bidding farewell to the city that had not shown her kindness. A city that brushed itself past her with no notice of the dream that she carried deep in her heart and mind. The city that refused to afford an opportunity for her. Goodbye.

Aneni had introspected long and hard of her future, especially after the two-hundred-dollar ordeal. She resorted to moving on to another province, still within Mozambique. Her plan was to go to Nampula, one of the cities in the north. She had heard that there may be more need for English teaching as it was in the remote part of the country with less exposure to the global world. However, Aneni did not have enough travel money to reach Nampula. She resorted to go through Zambezia Province, in Quelimane, as a temporary step until she could raise enough more money for her travel expenses to proceed to Nampula.

She packed her stuff in two bags and some in shopping bags. She felt so poor and disappointed that her dream may as well be coming to an end. She contemplated how long she had stayed in a foreign country, and all she could manage was to pack her belongings in a plastic bag. She set sail with no direction. She did not know anyone in Quelimane, but she held in her the unwavering hope that somehow, she would be fine.

She boarded *Chapa cem*, an omnibus to Quelimane. She had cried a lot the night before as she felt hollow and sad that life seemed to be throwing her to the curb no matter how much she tried to live right and work hard. She settled well on the bus, but the trip was nothing short of adventurous. The bus broke down after a hundred kilometres of departing from Beira, in the middle of Gorongosa. Aneni had quickly made friends with the other passengers on the omnibus to minimise loneliness and boredom. They warmed up to her because she spoke very fine English, and she always had a smile on her face. The driver advised passengers to stay put on the bus as it was a dangerous area due to dangerous animals running around. One of the other young Mozambican girls in the bus had some muffins and popcorn, which she gladly shared with everyone. A middle-aged man, who appeared a bit pompous by flaunting his job and salary he earned in a private company, seemed generous too as he provided everyone on the bus with orange juice. Aneni did not have anything to eat. At that moment, she slightly felt like a charity case, but again she quickly brushed it off and focused on the pressing matter like the broken bus.

It appeared the problem with the bus was bigger than what any of the people on the bus could manage. The breakdown crew who were supposed to sort out the problem arrived four hours later. The long wait was making people impatient. When the mechanic arrived, he managed to fiddle with the engine, in no time, the bus gave a signal of life. Excitement loomed in the bus as if after a continuous draught, a farmer saw the first drops of rain.

The day was coming to an end as the sun was setting. Suddenly, a smell of fresh water covered the bus. They arrived at the Zambezi River, which settled in a vast terrain, conjoined to a pebble riverbank, the river flowing silently, almost unrecognisable. There was a buzz of activity on either side of the river as the fishermen were busy recasting their nets for the morning catch. Nearby villagers were vending, shopping and drinking alcohol at the shebeens.

Zambezi River was between the South and the North of Mozambique. For cars and people to cross the river on to the other side, it required the services of a pontoon. The pontoon operated between seven in the morning to five in the evening. This meant that when their bus arrived, they could no longer cross onto the other side as it was late. Aneni and the other passengers would have to wait. Aneni's heart sank, it was humid, and the heat was unbearable. She imagined the night on a bus with other strangers although the strangers had become family along the journey. Due to the climate, the heat and the humidity, the area was mosquito prone which made it difficult for anyone to catch sleep with mosquitos buzzing and biting all the time.

The middle-aged man on the bus continued to be generous and bought everyone some food from the local canteen. The young girl on the bus resorted to singing to keep herself entertained. People chatted until they ran out of stories. Miraculously, dawn descended on the banks of Zambezi, and the hope of crossing the river and finally getting to their destination has awakened.

Upon crossing the Zambezi, they set sail Quelimane bound and suddenly a wave of fear and sadness covered Aneni's mind. She had no place to live, and she had no idea where she was going, let alone where she would sleep that night. She had contemplated asking some of her bus family, but she was apprehensive for some strange reason. Quelimane was a well-known coconut hub, and as the bus approached the town, the shadows of beautiful coconut trees waved into the bus. The amazing greenery was more pronounced as they entered the town. They arrived towards sunset. Aneni took her bags, including her plastic bags, bid farewell to her bus family and went her way.

She looked for a place to temporarily leave her bags while she sought accommodation for the night in Quelimane. The people were generous at a local, small café. It was a public place, so she felt somehow her luggage would be safe there as the people working there would notice if someone tried to steal it.

Aneni went around looking for a room to rent, although she did not have a lot of money. She got to a home where she was greeted by a mixed-race lady who appeared to be in her fifties. Aneni told her that she was looking for a room to rent and that she was South African looking for an English teaching job.

"It's too late for you to be looking for a house at this time. You can sleep here and look for a place tomorrow," the lady said. Aneni was elated by that news. She thanked the lady and told her that she needed to pick up her stuff from the local café. The lady asked her teenage daughter to escort her.

The hospitality at Dona Gilda's house was nothing short of amazing. They warmed her some water to bath and prepared very delicious food, coconut rice with crab soup and lettuce. She was given her bed to sleep in the same room as her teenage daughter.

In the morning, Dona Gilda told her that she could stay another day while she helped her to look for a place to rent. Aneni, being a well-cultured young lady, blended well with the family and helped around the house chores and talking with immense respect to everyone there.

Quelimane was a laid-back small town, community-oriented, everyone knew everyone's business and most were family. The town was dominated by the Chuabo's, who spoke mostly Portuguese. The representation of the mixed-race population was high, and their last names were mostly Portuguese. It was a warm town, with very warm and generous people.

Dona Gilda sat with her in the evening to announce that she had found a temporary room for her to rent, and the price was so low, and it fit her meagre savings. She went to see the room, which was immensely dilapidated and had a funny smell in it. The landlord had put in a small hard bed for Aneni to sleep in. Aneni had no choice but to take the room as a temporary measure.

As usual, she would wake up and go around looking for customers for her English teaching. One day, she knocked at a door and she was greeted by a very tall and handsome young man named Isak. Isak immediately refined his gaze when he saw this young, beautiful lady standing at his door. Aneni changed her agenda and instead she said that she was looking for a place to rent. She felt shy and embarrassed to say that she was looking for clients to teach English. Isak replied that he did not know but would like to help her look. He wanted her to tell him where she was currently living. She told him about the place and explained how uncomfortable it was. Aneni left with no hope of seeing him again as she did not think he meant it when he mentioned helping her.

The impact of masquerading as a South African was reaping results. The treatment and respect Aneni got from people after mentioning that was quite superb. Within, Aneni felt an immense sense of guilt and discomfort, but on the other hand, she had no option but to continue with the lie to see if that could get her where she wanted to be.

Chapter 14

It took no time until Aneni had secured some students for English teaching in Quelimane. She diligently attended her sessions in people's homes on time. She strengthened her teaching methods by using an old model radio that she found at the dilapidated house. Those types of small radios were called *Xirico*. There were some radio channels from the neighbouring country Malawi that used the English language in their programmes. She would use that for her comprehension lessons. It worked and in no time, she had stolen the hearts of her students and their families. Often, they would invite her to family events, lunches and dinners.

All of a sudden, life began to make sense. The people of Quelimane were the warmest. They had a strong spirit of humanity in them, which surprisingly made Aneni abandon her plans to proceed to Nampula. She felt so much at home.

One day she visited the local university in pursuit of an opportunity to conduct English teaching for a fee. She got to the reception and confidently asked if she could see the director of the university. The receptionist, Stella, asked her to wait as the director was busy. She patiently waited while Stella drew some interest in the way that Aneni was speaking in a poised, polished manner. She began to ask her a bit about her life and about her country South Africa. Stella also told her that she was a very beautiful girl, and she would most likely find a job teaching English in no time. Aneni was a bit taken aback by the connotation and link about her beauty and finding a job. In her mind, Aneni never thought she would use her body to get anywhere in life as she believed in attaining success through sheer hard work.

Stella called the director and announced that there was a young lady who wanted to speak to him.

"Olaa, tudo bem?" the director, Afonso, said. As Aneni set eyes on Afonso, words failed her. He was tall, dark, handsome and very friendly. She had expected to see an old man with a big belly, bald with glasses on. This to her was too much to take in. Afonso offered her to take a seat in front of his prestigious desk. Aneni became nervous but immediately controlled herself by remembering the main reason she was there.

At this time, she had changed her name to sound South African, and she was now introducing herself as Noma Mabena, short for Nomathamsanga. She introduced herself and told the director that she wanted to have a base at the university to teach English to the public. Teaching at a central location would be great for Aneni as it would reduce various trips to people's houses. She would also have a better job with more prestige and posture.

Director Afonso looked at Aneni in admiration caused by hearing an idea like that from a very young, beautiful girl.

"That is a great and noble idea," he said. "I would like you to meet our English lecturer," he added. Afonso called in the English lecturer to his office and discussed at length the possibility of Aneni doing English lessons at the university. The English lecturer agreed that it was a great idea.

"She is indeed a beautiful girl," Afonso remarked in Portuguese to the other English lecturer as he was leaving his office. He probably thought she would not catch the phrase, but she could not miss that one.

What is happening to me?, thought Aneni as she lay looking up at the ceiling in her very uncomfortable bed that night. She was happy at the possibility of having a place to teach English, but she wondered where this sudden wave of handsome men appearing in her life came from.

The days that followed were full of visits to the university to check the progress of her proposal. Surprisingly, her visits had something more than just for the premises for English teaching. She had started to enjoy seeing Afonso and talking to him. His English was very bad, but with the Portuguese that Aneni had learnt, they were able to communicate.

Despite the instant infatuation that Aneni felt for Afonso, she did not derail from her plans. She wanted to hold in her hands the dream she always yearned for, and not even a handsome man could take that dream away.

In the weeks that followed, Aneni kept to her monotonous schedule, and soon word had gone out that there was a young and beautiful English teacher in the community. Of course, Aneni was so used to this remark since her attempt at life in Manica.

One day, Aneni received a call from Afonso to announce that there was an English teaching vacancy with the medium institute of the university, and Afonso wanted her to commence as soon as possible. This was the greatest news Aneni had ever received. She was summoned to the administration office to sign a contract. She left the office in an elated mood, so elated that she decided to take a solitary walk around town so she could deflate her excitement.

While she took her walk, thanking God for the blessings, she bumped into Isak. He seemed quite excited to see Aneni.

"I have been looking for you. How have you been?" Isak asked with a beaming smile on his face.

"Oh hi," she mumbled, surprised at the sudden meeting. "I've been around. How are you?"

"I found you a place to rent near the town. It's nicer than where you are living. Would you like to go and see it?" he asked. She could see the excitement in his eyes.

"Of course. Let's go and see it," she answered, unable to conceal her own excitement.

The room was an outside cottage, fully furnished with a nice single bed with new pink linen and a small table with two chairs at the far end of the bed. The toilet and bathroom were outside, clean and tidy. The set-up took to Aneni's fancy and she felt another wave of excitement that she could not explain, not even to herself. The landlord said she would want a deposit to guarantee the rental. Aneni did not have it, but Isak said he would help her pay for it.

In an instant, it all seemed surreal for Aneni to be in an exciting mode and this was the first time since she had crossed the border into Mozambique to be completely happy. The bud of achieving her dreams was rebirthing in a town she intended not to stay which turned out to be home for her.

Weeks passed, and Aneni had happily settled into her new room and her new job. She did not stop giving her house tuition classes, and it became her side hustle, making enough to start saving money.

As the month was drawing nigh, Aneni was summoned to the office at her new job to provide her qualifications. She only had on her the high school Ordinary Level certificates, which she could not use. She had used a different name and country of origin to introduce herself to the school. Suddenly she became sombre, unsure of what to do. She told the officer that she would bring them in a week.

Aneni went to speak to Juliana, a young lady who worked in one of the local internet cafes. Juliana spoke excellent English, and Aneni would frequent the internet café to check her emails, she had built a good rapport with her over time. She humbly asked her for a favour and the favour required her to design a forged certificate to present to the university. Aneni convincingly presented her case. She related that she had lost her certificates and needed some help with designing a simple one she could use for her new job. On the certificate, she put her South African name, Nomathamsanga Mabena.

Juliana let out a smirk, a friendly one, which announced to Aneni that it was okay and that she would help her. Within two days, the certificates were done. One was for Advanced Level qualifications, passed with flying colours, and the second one was a certificate for English Teaching as a Foreign Language. The certificates looked perfect, and Aneni was convinced that they would be accepted by the university. Aneni made copies of the certificates, carefully putting them in the envelope and rendered them to the admin at her new job.

A sigh of relief came over her as she left the admin block to attend one of her classes. The guilt within her continued as Aneni felt that she was representing a fake person to the community that had so far welcomed and warmed up immensely to her. She thought of bible scriptures she had read about incidences in which God allowed people to lie for a good cause. She recalled the lie that Abraham made, disguising his wife as his sister to spare them in difficult times. Lying was not contented upon in society, neither by her biblical principles, but she comforted herself by realising she had no other way out into her dream. Perhaps God had allowed this lie to make her make a positive difference in her life.

Life continued in a sweet, smooth manner as it had never felt before. Her new experiences in Quelimane pronounced a perfect life, a life full of hope and excitement. The lessons were going well at the university and her charisma and charm had yet again gained her love and high regard from those she worked with and her students. She put extra effort into the standard and quality of her English teaching with the inclusion of television and radio sessions.

One day, Aneni visited Afonso's office just to get feedback on how she was doing and to express her gratitude for the opportunity he had awarded her. Strangely, Aneni's infatuation for Afonso had sort of vanquished, her life had suddenly become busy, and she had to uphold a professional demeanour in the community.

However, Afonso's charm was so persistent such that at times, his approach was difficult to resist. On that day, he wrote an invite for Aneni to attend a musical by a local drama group called *Montes Namuli*. It was going to be centred on Shakespear's play, *Romeo and Juliet*. The sound of an invite from him was so romantic and Aneni felt a special kind of feeling, that feeling one can only get from a special person. She accepted the invite and told him that she would love to attend.

On the day of the theatre drama, Aneni carefully picked a three-quarter length African print skirt and a tight half sleeve body top. She also put on her best sandals. Her hair was braided neatly, and she put on some very light make-up and perfume. The clothes shaped her very beautiful silhouette. She always remembered to put on her shiny, beautiful smile, which let out gentleness, charm and sweetness.

Aneni felt that her life was taking shape by being a local pre-medium university lecturer. It gave her a different posture in society, and at twenty years old, she felt she was ready to carry the world on her shoulders.

Aneni exuded confidence, maturity, self-determination and purpose that any person who came in contact with her would rarely miss. Her hunger for success grounded her and kept her in line.

Outside the theatre, people were greeting each other and laughing at jokes. Some were just hanging out with their friends, waiting for the organising team to usher them into the theatre. Aneni went straight to the door as she knew no one, so she wanted to find a seat and settle. Aneni was friendly but she sometimes let out shyness in social settings where she was not familiar with the people. As she entered the door, Afonso saw her and came to her beaming a grand smile. In Mozambican culture, people kiss on both cheeks in greeting. This was quite unusual for Aneni. As Afonso leaned forward to kiss her on the cheek, a wave of passion and infatuation descended upon her once again, and for a moment, she felt her body and morals betraying her. She looked at Afonso to notice that the top part of his shirt was unbuttoned. The slight peep made her feel even more infatuated since she saw him only in professional settings so far.

Afonso led Aneni to her seat and asked how she was doing.

"I am fine. I am happy to be here," she responded, a little shyly, after the little encounter at the door.

"That's great. I do hope you enjoy every bit. Let me proceed to welcome some of the attendants," Afonso said while patting Aneni on the shoulder. His palm lingered on her skin for a second, and she felt as if she had stopped breathing.

People settled, and Aneni could not dismiss the intimate moment that she had just encountered with Afonso. As she was wallowing and drowning in the very pleasant thoughts of his charm. Afonso appeared on stage holding a small piece of paper. Sitting properly to pay attention, Aneni looked at Afonso's hands. With great dismay, she realised that Afonso had a gold band on his finger. Wedding ring. Aneni felt stupid and disappointed in herself for allowing Afonso to appear in her thoughts.

At that point, she realised Afonso was a no-go area, and whatever feelings she had for him had to be erased immediately. The drama finished and as good as it was, Aneni was mourning the short-lived excitement she had had just a few moments prior.

Chapter 15

Aneni received a call from the university early Monday morning. The weather was hot and humid. She had woken up early to prepare her lesson plans. The call was from the admin office. They were asking Aneni to have her certificates certified by authorities in order for her paycheque to be issued. This news came as a shock. Aneni had since forgotten about doing any more clandestine activities to prove her genuineness. A genuineness that was not.

Aneni knew that her certificates were not genuine, and they would not pass to be certified. A dark cloud had suddenly reigned upon her, threatening to take away the happiness and comfort that she had just found.

"Yes, I will get them certified," she said before ending the call. Tears started welling down her smooth cheeks upon realising that getting out of this one would be close to impossible.

Aneni scrolled down her Motorola phone, which her landlord had given to her because her daughter had bought her a new one. In the phone contacts, she checked on people who could help her with this issue. During the time that Aneni had socially interacted in Quelimane, she was introduced to so many people at events and outings. Some of the contacts had very high-ranking positions in government, having a strong influence in society. She had met the family of the Provincial Director of Agriculture, whose wife, Raima was so humble and warm that she immediately warmed up to Aneni. Raima had on occasions invited Aneni for lunch or dinner, and at times to her home to learn a few English words and chat.

Aneni went to the university to get her documents. As she was leaving with her certificates clasped under her arms, Afonso offered to let the school driver take her to the offices where the certification was to take place. She immediately dismissed him and said she would be fine on her own. *Going with the school driver would surely complicate things*, she thought. Aneni called Raima to check if she was home, and Raima said yes.

"There is something urgent that I want to talk to you about," Aneni said on the phone, and Raima invited her over. She walked in a hurry, coupled with panic and anxiety. She could see her life derailing back to misery, and Raima was her only hope. Her eyes were full of tears when she arrived at Raima's.

"Aneni, what is going on?" Raima asked her.

"Raima, I need to have these certificates certified. I left the originals back home in South Africa, and I can't have them certified without the originals. Is there any way you can help me?"

"Oh, Aneni, let me put on my shoes. We can go and talk to one of the ladies I know who works there. Let's see what she says," Raima offered, and within minutes, they were on their way. While on their way to the offices, Aneni held her heart on the sleeve. The outcome of this mess would either destroy her or build her. They arrived at the offices and rushed to the room where Raima's friend worked.

Raima had asked if Aneni had some money on her. Aneni gladly surrendered the twenty Meticals that she had left in her purse. Raima took the certificates from her, confidently handing them to the lady that she had mentioned.

"We have these certificates for my young sister that need to be certified." While she handed in the certificates, she also discreetly handed in the twenty Meticals. Within two minutes, the certificates were certified. Aneni cried from within because she was overwhelmed with joy. She could not thank Raima enough. *How could a 'thank you' explain what I mean and feel right now?*

The hurdle was done, and two days later, Aneni received her paycheque. The figures were quite attractive, and she started calculating how much of those paycheques she needed for her dream to be realised. It appeared she would need to stay a little longer than expected for that to happen, but she didn't mind. She looked at the cheque again and realised that she needed identity documents that matched the name that was on the cheque. Aneni did not have any documents except her Zimbabwean identity document and birth certificate, which could not suffice.

And, just like that, she was facing another issue. Without any identification, she would not be able to get the money that she worked for from the bank. She felt the downside of fake representation - it often required a million other fake representations to sustain.

Again, Aneni found herself numb such that even the energy to pray had vanished. She felt that praying for God to help her do illegal activities was more of a mockery of her Maker than putting him on his supreme pedestal.

Aneni decided not to lose sleep over it, but rather, she had to gather the courage to go and cash the cheque with as much confidence as she could. The following morning, just as the banks were opening, Aneni was there in a small queue with her beloved cheque clasped firmly in her hands.

She quickly studied the environment and remembered that she needed to carry a kind smile, very gentle and sweet.

The male teller called her through. She greeted him with a lot of respect, and used polished English, hoping that it would disguise her lack of identification.

"Good morning, sir. I would like to cash in my cheque, but my passport has been sent to immigration for my visa," she said and smiled, looking the teller in the eyes. "I am an English lecturer at the local university. Can you please help me?" She had her head slightly tilted to her left as a gesture of humbleness and plea. The teller greeted her back and immediately cashed in the cheque.

"Have a good day ma'am," he said after handing Aneni her hard-earned cash. This became the norm for the next twelve months in which Aneni received her paycheques. The same teller would gladly attend to her and give her money without asking a single question of identification.

Quelimane had become the sun that rose and seized to set for Aneni. The way things had happened, she could not comprehend how that could have been. She thought one day, with tears in her eyes, *could this be God who has strategically positioned his angels to help me?* It surely made no sense to her that she had managed to manipulate the law so much and was not questioned in any way. She was convinced in herself that finally, God was working his miracle in her life. If this was a miracle, then her dream should be achievable too.

The first semester at university was ending mid-summer. Most lecturers were inundated and drowning in exam preparation, marking and invigilation. Aneni had finished her exam preparation. She was marking and submitting the results to the university exam board. She had an impeccable work ethic, and she tried to put her all into the way she taught her students. She was ever so full of self-determination, purpose and focus. She, however, did not want to rest on her laurels, and the break of the semester meant she needed to have a plan in place to keep her work going.

Aneni went back to Afonso to enquire about the plan to have private English lessons for the general public during the three-month semester break. Afonso concurred with her plan and gave her the go-ahead to use the university as a base for her private English lessons. Aneni worked hard to promote the English lessons. She would send letters to private organisations and government institutions. She even went to the local radio to promote her classes. She patiently waited every day in a deserted room within the university for registrations.

The first week passed without many events, just a few enquiries and a few phone calls. The second and third week, the enquiries grew in leaps and bounds, and she could not contain them. The Ministry of Health called her, which had thirty employees in need of lessons. Then ten employees from the Ministry of Tourism joined in. In no time, her capacity was overflowing, and she could not contain all of them. Payments were being made promptly for the three-month intensive English lessons.

In no time, Aneni had amassed a little wealth of her own, which would amount to four thousand United States Dollars converted from Meticals. It was surreal - at last, her dream would come true.

Aneni kept her money in the house because she could not open a bank account without identity documents.

The fear had started to creep in at the possibility of it being stolen. It was not a bother before, because there wasn't much of it, but at this rate, with what she was earning from the private lessons, she needed water-tight storage for her treasure.

Her friendship with Raima unlocked possibilities on a grand scale. Through her, she was able to connect to the registrar, who was responsible for the entire province registry office. Senhor Mariano was a stout, tall and intimidating man. He was known to keep his circles very tight as a way of avoiding corrupt favours. *I don't think he can smile,* Aneni thought. He had a beautiful family and was quite committed to his role as a father, except, as Aneni later found out, he also had a younger girlfriend who was always in the background.

When Aneni was introduced to him by Raima and her husband, she was intimidated. Raima asked on her behalf if Senhor Mariano could help Aneni get Mozambican particulars.

"She can talk to Joana about this. She is my secretary, and she can help her," he responded in a stern, dry way. That was all he said, and nothing else was needed, no further probing or interest to know the reason behind the favour. It did not bother Aneni as she was focused on getting what she wanted.

The following Monday, Aneni was early to get to the registrar's office. The secretary received her very warmly and mentioned the orders she had received from her boss. She started the process for Aneni to have her identity document. She cited that she had no birth certificate and her parents had died before making one. The secretary looked at her with a smile that suggested she knew she was lying but being under the wing of an influential man meant brushing it off and smiling. Aneni used her new name, the South African name and surname, mainly because it matched her other fake particulars. Another wave of guilt and pain was inevitable for Aneni, upon realising that she was harnessing a fake identity. When she got home, she cried bitterly, but at the same time, there was a kind of inner happiness that she would conduct her dealings properly.

After three weeks, Aneni's identity documents came, and she went straight to open a bank account.

Back home, Aneni's family was beginning to get worried about her. They were not entirely sure whether she was okay and if the plan to achieve her dreams was working. Time had passed with no sign of it happening. One of her eldest brothers had raised a concern that she could potentially end up in prostitution if things did not fall into place as expected. Many theories and worries surfaced.

Communication was difficult, and at the time, the mobile phone wave was not as rampant, it was confined to the very rich in society. Neither did Aneni's family own a telephone line - it was a very distant luxury to even imagine having it. The only communication she could make was with her older sister as her husband's family owned a landline telephone. On two occasions, she was able to speak to her mum while she was visiting her sister. The emotion of hearing her mum's voice was always overwhelming, and most times, she would let out tears of both happiness and sadness after she was done. Sadness because she missed her and would have wanted to see her more regularly; happiness because of the nostalgia of the good times spent at the farm. However, she knew she was doing the right thing by following her dream. She was doing it not only for herself but also for her parents. *One day, they will understand,* she thought to herself, as tears fell down her face after a very touching phone call.

Chapter 16

Aneni's infatuation for Afonso had completely died down. She continued to pursue her dream, working hard each day. Her warmth and friendliness afforded her many outings from friends who thought the world of her. She had suddenly become the talk of the town as being the most peculiar English teacher to ever grace the land of Quelimane. Her prowess soared as many of her students, especially the private ones, came out of the course speaking almost fluent English, which had never happened before with other teachers.

Isak had also disappeared into thin air. They had only met a few more times after helping Aneni find a house, and that was it. She paid him back for the deposit, and she never saw him again. In the wave of her success, he never appeared again. Aneni felt strongly that the Supreme Being had strategically positioned angels to carry her through the hurdles that laid ahead. In her prayers, she would always remember all the people who played a pivotal role in attaining her success.

Life was great, Aneni met a young engineer at a dinner party which she was invited to as a very important guest by her friend Nilsa. The engineer was called Sergio and had professed to have taken immediate attraction to Aneni when he saw her seated, quietly observing everyone at the party. He particularly mentioned that he was captivated by her calmness and her modest yet appealing dress.

At the end of the party, the young engineer offered her a lift with his friends. She hesitated a little as there were three men in that car.

"Are you sure this is okay?" she asked Nilsa.

"These are very nice guys. I vouch for them. You will be safe," she said with a smirk. The distance to Aneni's house was not very long. Before Sergio could chat her up on anything else apart from small talk, they had already arrived at her home. Sergio stood by the gate, asking for Aneni's number. With slight hesitation, the play-hard-to-get kind, Aneni reluctantly gave him her number. He had to write on his arm because his phone battery was off, and there was no paper in sight. She found that quite endearing.

The following morning, Sergio rang.

"Do you remember me?" That was his introduction. His English was not too good but enough to understand her and strike a conversation.

"Yes, I do remember you," she responded. That same evening Sergio asked Aneni to go out for a walk at the water marginal. It was a very tranquil place, overlooking a river, the peace it brought and the wind which offered a cold embrace without asking for permission.

The conversation was great. They spoke about personal dreams and aspirations, they spoke about family, and Aneni continued with her lie of being South African. She felt that it was too early for her to let the cat out of the bag, she did not know Sergio enough. In fact, she didn't know him at all, even if it felt like they had known each other for a long time. After the beautiful walk, they went to dinner and proceeded to their respective homes after eating.

The moments came flashing as Aneni laid her head on the pillow. She felt good about herself. She was confident that Sergio had fallen immediately for her. Aneni's charm was impeccable, she was soft, hardworking, young and ambitious. A very rare kind of woman she was.

In the days that followed, their encounters together became regular as the calls and messages became a daily routine. Aneni laid out her aspiration to remain chaste until she was committed to someone fully, and Sergio could not have been more enchanted.

Sergio respected Aneni's desire and choice to not engage in sexual activities before marriage. He would even take Aneni away on holidays, and still, he never crossed the boundary. Their relationship was strong, and although Aneni did not want to get married at twenty-one, Sergio was already making plans to marry her. He did not want to lose out on such a wonderful woman. Introductions were made to his family, and they welcomed her with open arms.

Days passed into weeks and months, the relationship remained intact and not at all shaken. It was amazing. Sergio was getting serious about them. The boundaries were kept in check, and Aneni continued to make a success out of her English classes.

On one fateful day, Sergio asked Aneni if he could be introduced to her family, at least one person, just in case anything happens to her. This came after Sergio had sniffed concerns regarding her background. He had noticed a lot of grey areas in her stories, which he was hesitant to probe or speak about as he feared it could've been a sensitive topic. The main grey area was her failure to comprehend and speak any South African language. Over time, he had noticed her avoidance of any conversation related to her childhood. She had never made calls home in his presence, which made him even more suspicious. At the time, their relationship was so tight that they spent most of their free time together. His love for her made it extremely difficult for him to address his thoughts - he preferred her to open up voluntarily.

The subject of her family brought in some tension in their relationship. Aneni was not willing to divulge the truth to Sergio, neither did she feel she would want to marry him. Although he was a very poised and responsible eligible bachelor, Aneni felt that his urge to marry would deter her from achieving and executing her aspirations and dreams. At least at the time, she was not ready at all to marry.

Sergio soon realised that Aneni was not ready to commit to the relationship, and she was still not willing to confide in him. The excitement they once shared gradually died down, Aneni would make excuses not to see him. She was also beginning to feel the discomfort of knowing that Sergio realised that she was a mystery. If he knew, who else suspected?

Chapter 17

Speculation about Aneni masquerading under a false name were starting to surface as one of the ladies that Aneni knew in Manica transferred to Quelimane. Upon meeting Aneni at the university, she shouted her real name. After that, she talked to other people who worked at the university, making comments about all the good work that Aneni did in her town.

"For a girl from Zimbabwe, she's very hard-working and intelligent," she would say, ruining Aneni's reputation. Her university colleagues began to ask Aneni questions about her background. The discomfort became unbearable.

Aneni went back to her Maker and prayed, believing that God was urging her to make a move which is why suddenly her life was becoming tense.

Upon reflection, Aneni felt that it was time, time to go, time for goodbyes. Everything good and great must eventually come to an end - that's how life was constructed. Comfort zones appeared to shatter after a while.

Aneni officially ended her relationship with Sergio, painfully so. Sergio was quite disturbed and heartbroken, but Aneni felt it was for the best. She wanted free space to navigate her next adventure without the need to involve anyone else. Her bank balance was healthy. She had managed to raise enough to renovate her parents' home and pursue her dream to go to the United Kingdom in search of greener pastures. She planned to exchange the Meticals into United Stated Dollars, pack her bags and bid farewell to her students, her colleagues and friends who had made her life beautiful during her stay in Quelimane.

Farewells were always painful. The night before she left Quelimane, Aneni read a poem over dinner organised by her friends. The poem was written by Eugenio Tavares in 1969. It was a poem dedicated to families whose children left Cabo Verde in search of greener pastures abroad. It signified the pain for the future unknown of their children, who used boats to cross rivers and seas to other bays. There was no guarantee of them making it alive or seeing each other again. It signified hope - if pastures green abounds, then tears of joy would suffice. Aneni repeated the poem to herself many times after leaving Quelimane.

Morna de Despedida

Time to part
Time of pain
My desire
That it does not dawn
Each time
I remember
I prefer
To stay and die

Time to part
Time of pain
Love
Let me cry
Captive soul
You leave, you are a slave
The soul that lives
I will take you

When the arrival is sweet
The parting is bitter
If we do not part, but who does not part
You do not return, do not return
If we die
At parting
In God's coming
Life he will give us

Let me cry
Destiny of men
Oh pain
Without a name
Pain of love
Pain of fondness
Of someone
Whom I want, who wants me

Let me cry
Destiny of men
Oh pain
Without a name
Suffering together with you
Without certainty
Dying in the absence
With your sadness

(Eugenio Tavares, 1969)

"In this house called earth, navigating the river of time, have as an oar my love, and friendship", Aneni spoke with tears welling down her cheeks. These words became the seal and the signature of this chapter of her life. Mozambique had brought her tears and fears, love and laughter, failure and success. This chapter represented a bag full of profound, meaningful life lessons. As with everything that started well, it ought to end well.

Aneni embraced and kissed her friends in a bid of farewell. Tears welled down their cheeks, presents were shared. Sergio wept the most. Despite the end of their relationship, Sergio still had immense love for Aneni. However, it was time, time to let go and open a new chapter without him in it.

At the dawn of the day of her departure, Aneni got ready quickly. Sergio and some of her friends had offered to take her to the bus. This time around, Aneni felt proud that she would cross for the first time the border the proper way, not the clandestine way she had come in. The Mozambicans and Zimbabweans forged a no visa rule for either citizens. This meant Aneni would go back to Zimbabwe as a Mozambican, carrying a South African name. Many times, Aneni had brushed the very painful thought of how much of a mess her identity was. The excitement of seeing her mum and dad, her siblings and nieces was insurmountable. Almost three and a half years, Aneni had not seen her family and she only spoke with them a few times.

She had bought clothes and souvenirs for her family, not to mention that she had amassed enough money to spare to renovate her parents' home. She immediately remembered the day when it rained so much in the middle of the night that her mum had woken up to ask her to move from where she was sleeping in fear of the house falling on her. She remembered it with much pain, but at the same instant, she held on to the happiness that she was finally armoured to put that shame to an end. Throughout her journey, she also envisioned her life at the very top and fulfilling her dreams in the United Kingdom. The ten thousand United States Dollars was enough to take her there. But first, she had to see her family.

The trip from Quelimane to the Forbes border post was about eight hours long, which meant by two in the afternoon Aneni was hailing at the border, and for the first time, getting her passport stamped. In preparation to cross the border, people had advised that she does not put all her money in one place so that she would not attract the customs declaration of funds. She strategically hid the money under her shoes, toiletry bag and in her brassier.

The border was bustling, with cross border traders making a mark for themselves by carrying unique bags with goods and materials for sale. Aneni was perplexed at the overconfidence of some of the traders. They spoke as if they owned the border and knew everything.

"Make sure you have a few dollars to pay customs if you don't want to be delayed," one of them said to Aneni. This only brought more anxiety than excitement to Aneni, as she chose to ignore and look away. A group of young men were holding wads of Meticals and dollars, pestering every person passing by the border to change their money with them.

"I have a good rate. How much do you want?" they would ask. The more Aneni told them she did not need any, the more they pushed further, promising to give an even better deal. It was too much commotion. And there were also monkeys that were threatening to grab people's food and bags. Aneni made sure she clasped her purse tightly under her arm.

In the line to stamp the passport, the commotion continued as the truck drivers would push to get priority. Chaos ensued, but Aneni held on to her passport, knowing fully well that she was going back home to see her beloved family.

After all the bureaucracy at the border, Aneni was safely on the other side, now feeling the smell of her motherland, killing nostalgia as the poetry of success embroiled her.

Aneni arrived home as the sun was starting to set. She announced her arrival by calling her mum.

"Mummy, mummy! I'm here." Mum, dad and her niece were in the kitchen preparing to eat dinner. No one knew that Aneni was coming home. When her niece Kora heard her calling, she ran out of the kitchen to see who it was.

"Aunty Ane!" Kora called out and ran towards Aneni to embrace her. MaMushambi and VaMushambi followed with excitement. They embraced and let out tears of joy and immense happiness.

The family was swept by emotion - her dad even abandoned his food because of the excitement of seeing her.

"You look well, my daughter. We missed you," he said.

"I missed you so much too. How is everyone doing around?" she asked. The conversations carried on for the greater part of the night. Some parts were painful as she would learn about the suffering and deaths of people she knew in the area. Some were funny and exciting, especially the news of her friends who got married and had kids. By the time they went to sleep, the corks were already crowing, announcing the start of dawn, the start of a new day.

In the following morning, dad went to the local call box to ring her sister, announcing Aneni's return. He further advised her sister to notify everyone to come home to see Aneni for the weekend. Her brothers, sisters and nieces came. Two goats were killed for a feast, and people rejoiced and sang hymns of praise throughout the night.

Aneni made her plans known to the family. She told them that she wanted to renovate her parents' house. She also made sure to say that she would be pursuing her dream to proceed to the United Kingdom. The news was received with much gratitude and happiness, prayers and blessings from the family followed.

In almost no time, the renovation was completed. Her mum was in awe as her dream of having a house with an arch had finally come to fruition. Aneni felt happy and content within herself for having done something noble for her beloved parents. She was finally seeing the results of years of hard work, and she could not help but shed a single tear.

Chapter 18

Three months after coming back home, Aneni left the village. She went straight to Harare, the capital city of Zimbabwe. She was hosted at her sister Mudiwa's matrimonial home in Belvedere, the northern suburbs of Harare, where she used to make calls when she was in Mozambique. She aimed to get a Zimbabwean passport immediately and pursue a visa to go to the United Kingdom.

The weather was cool. At the onset of winter, the fresh breeze would kiss Aneni's cheeks in the morning as she got ready to get into town to crack on with her passport application. Anesu, the last-born girl in the family, was also living with Mudiwa. She was there helping Mudiwa take care of her baby Ruvimbo. Aneni had wanted to see her young sister Anesu do well in life. She was not very academically gifted, but Aneni felt that she needed exposure in identifying her capabilities in the skills department. She had in passing mentioned her love and passion for the beauty industry but with the situation hailing in Zimbabwe, the business had ceased to be as lucrative as before because people of no other professions resorted to that kind of business as a last resort.

"Can you get ready to go the passport offices with me? I want you to also apply for your passport," Aneni said to Anesu as she folded wands of United States Dollars into a tiny purse.

"Alright, I will bathe and get ready in a few minutes," Anesu responded, rushing to get a bucket for bathing. Anesu was very excited as passports were like golden dust at that time in Zimbabwe. Many could not afford and manage to get them. The wave of people yearning for greener pastures had made millions require passports urgently, which made them more expensive.

"I want you to do something tangible in your life," Aneni said to her sister when they sat in the taxi. "To get exposure to bigger and better things. We did not have much growing up, but we do not want to have a poor future, do we?" she asked Anesu.

"Aneni, I want to do something better for myself. Maybe a beauty course and then I can look for a job in the neighbouring countries. It might be hard, but I want to do it. I want to follow my dream like you followed yours," she said and Aneni saw a flicker or familiar determination in her eyes. *She will do just fine*, she thought, with a small smile on her face.

The queue at the passport offices was unbelievable - there was a sea of people waiting their turn to get an application form.

"Well, this is just incredible," Aneni let out a sigh of discontentment. It had suddenly dawned on her that the journey of struggle was still far from over. The sadness appeared on the faces of many - the struggle to get a passport was real. Some mentioned that they had been coming to get a form for a week, and they always came out empty-handed. People were desperate to seek greener pastures in the diaspora, as the inflation rate in Zimbabwe was hitting an all-time high, which rendered the currency incompatible. Salaries had remained stagnant, while commodity prices were skyrocketing by the minute. Everyone wanted a better life that Zimbabwe could not provide. It pained her to see the once renowned breadbasket of Africa becoming a basket case.

Aneni called her brother Maguza, relaying the challenge presented right in front of her.

"Let me call someone who works there. I will let you know what they say," Maguza said while encouraging Aneni to be patient and not worry about it too much. The day passed, and there was no success and getting ahead. Her brother came to see her and Anesu in town.

"Can you not use the Mozambican passport to go to the UK instead? You may have less hustle with that than to pursue the Zimbabwean passport."

"No, brother. I want to get an education, and it has to be in my real name and nationality," she said. She was done with pretending to be someone else. Hollowness filled Aneni. Earlier, she was very excited, thinking that it was going to be an easy transition, but it was a hurdle. Still, she did not want to let the thoughts of discouragement linger in her mind.

"Tomorrow, you can go and meet a lady called mai Nhasi at the passport offices. She charges $250 per person for her services to expedite the process", Maguza said. Aneni felt a glimmer of hope in her heart.

"That's fine as long as the passports are guaranteed... Will they be guaranteed?"

"Yes."

"Good."

Aneni got a grey envelope. She put $500 in it and gave it to mai Nhasi. Nobody at the passport offices was supposed to know of this transaction, as mai Nhasi would lose her job, so it was done as discreetly as possible.

Mai Nhasi handed out the application forms. Aneni and Anesu filled them in quickly in her office. Together they handed the applications back to her with their passport photos.

"Come tomorrow afternoon to collect," Mai Nhasi said as they were leaving.

It wore Aneni that, even in her own country, she had to do certain things clandestinely to achieve her dream. She, however, dismissed the thought and chose to accept that it may be long until she could do things without having to rely on who knew who and how much she could pay for services. Corruption inevitably became rife in countries where people's income served only for the basics, at times even less. It was like being between a rock and a hard place, taking the jugular became the norm, a painful norm.

The next day Aneni had tears in her eyes as she looked at her green passport with her real name and nationality written on it. For a moment, she thought of discarding the Mozambican passport with a South African name. She decided to keep it so she could tell her story to her grandchildren in decades to come. It could serve as an exhibit of her hardships, evidence of what it took to reach her dreams.

Two days after getting her passport, Aneni immediately applied for a UK visa through a local agency. The first application was denied, on the grounds of the apparent high risk of her not returning to Zimbabwe. This came when a few Zimbabwean footballers had left for the UK to play football, only to disappear with no thoughts of coming back to Africa. Most of them ended up seeking asylum for a stay in the UK. It was devastating news for Aneni, but she did not want to give up. This dream was too big for her to let go of it. She had gone through so much to reach the point where she was, and to throw it all away was not an option. She also could not envision herself in any other African country as, at that time, her whole heart was taken by the United Kingdom. She sent another application, with a positive heart.

While waiting for the reply, Aneni had paid for Anesu to take a course in beauty therapy with the hope that once she settled in the UK, Anesu would follow.

A second application went through to the second stage of the process, this time with a different agency. The anxiety of waiting with uncertainty killed Aneni within, she could envision herself walking the streets of London. She preferred not to imagine her misery at the possibility of the refusal of a visa. Time went by. Two weeks felt like two years of being stuck in a state of anticipation.

Then, one day, Aneni received a call from the agency, requesting her to come to their offices immediately. She could not bathe, neither could she find the time to change into presentable clothes. What awaited her at the agency was of more importance than looking good.

She took a deep breath and opened the door to the office with desperation, only to see a beaming smile on the office administrator's face. Immediately she knew, God had answered her prayers. *This is it. This must be it. My visa must've been granted*, she thought.

Shelter handed a brown envelope to Aneni. With trembling hands, she opened the envelope and in it was her passport with a study visa to the United Kingdom. How this agency had managed it, she did not know as it only mattered that Aneni had been granted a visa to achieve her dream, going to study in the United Kingdom.

Her heart sung when she boarded the plane, her dream so close she could feel it on her skin.

Chapter 19

"Aneni Mushambi, Bachelor of Science Pharmacology Honours", the vice-chancellor of the University of Buckinghamshire echoed her name in an auditorium full of graduates, friends and families who had come to witness the graduation of their loved ones. In black regalia with a blue and white sash carefully set around her gown, Aneni looked nothing short of amazing, a smile beaming on her face while she took a proud step in high heels to receive her degree. She shook the chancellor's hand with a tight, reassuring yet professional grip, and she held her degree for the first time. While looking back at her journey, Aneni let out tears of joy as she thought of all the amazing people who had helped to get her where she was now.

The dream that was; the dream that became!